If the walls of Stockwell Mansion could talk…

We'd say good riddance to that curmudgeon Caine Stockwell. He's thrown his last crystal vase against us, that's for sure! When Caine was alive he did nothing but make piles of money and mountains of mischief. And it's beginning to look like that money and that mischief are *very* close cousins…. The Stockwell siblings recently uncovered some damning papers…documents that seem to verify that a Stockwell ancestor bilked his neighbors, the Johnsons, of their valuable land—fine Texas property oozing with black gold! Well, thank goodness the mean gene didn't pass down to any of *this* generation of Stockwells. They're all anxious to discover the truth and set things straight.

And no better man for the job than mercenary Jack Stockwell. He banished himself from his notorious family years ago, but is back for a last call of duty. Under an assumed name, he's working on Beth Johnson's storm-ravaged rose farm in order to dig up the dirt on the *dirt*. Seems Jack can't quite keep his attention on the ground, however—his mind's swirling with tantalizing thoughts of Beth!

In the search for their long-lost mother, the Stockwell siblings find a sister, too! But she barely steps foot in Texas when she's kidnapped—and rescued by a Prince Charming rancher in *The Cattleman and the Virgin Heiress*, SE #1393, by Jackie Merritt, available May 2001, only from Silhouette Special Edition.

Dear Reader,

When Patricia Kay was a child, she could be found hiding somewhere...reading. "Ever since I was old enough to realize someone wrote books and they didn't just magically appear, I dreamed of writing," she says. And this month Special Edition is proud to publish Patricia's twenty-second novel, *The Millionaire and the Mom,* the next of the STOCKWELLS OF TEXAS series. She admits it isn't always easy keeping her ideas and her writing fresh. What helps, she says, is "nonwriting" activities, such as singing in her church choir, swimming, taking long walks, going to the movies and traveling. "Staying well-rounded keeps me excited about writing," she says.

We have plenty of other fresh stories to offer this month. After finding herself in the midst of an armed robbery with a gun to her back in Christie Ridgway's *From This Day Forward,* Annie Smith vows to chase her dreams.... In the next of A RANCHING FAMILY series by Victoria Pade, Kate McDermot returns from Vegas unexpectedly married and with a *Cowboy's Baby* in her belly! And Sally Tyler Hayes's *Magic in a Jelly Jar* is what young Luke Morgan hopes for by saving his teeth in a jelly jar...because he thinks that his dentist is the tooth fairy and can grant him one wish: a mother! Also, don't miss the surprising twists in *Her Mysterious Houseguest* by Jane Toombs, and an exciting forbidden love story with Barbara Benedict's *Solution: Marriage.*

At Special Edition, fresh, innovative books are our passion. We hope you enjoy them all.

Best,

Karen Taylor Richman
Senior Editor

Please address questions and book requests to:
Silhouette Reader Service
U.S.: 3010 Walden Ave., P.O. Box 1325, Buffalo, NY 14269
Canadian: P.O. Box 609, Fort Erie, Ont. L2A 5X3

The Millionaire and the Mom

PATRICIA KAY

SPECIAL EDITION™

Published by Silhouette Books

America's Publisher of Contemporary Romance

Special thanks and acknowledgment are given to
Patricia Kay for her contribution
to the Stockwells of Texas series.

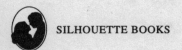

SILHOUETTE BOOKS

ISBN 0-373-24387-1

THE MILLIONAIRE AND THE MOM

Visit Silhouette at www.eHarlequin.com

Printed in U.S.A.

Books previously written as Trisha Alexander

PATRICIA KAY

has had a lifelong love affair with books and has always wanted to be a writer. She also loves cats, movies, the ocean, music, Broadway shows, cooking, traveling, being with her family and friends, Cajun food, "Calvin and Hobbes" and getting mail. Patricia and her husband have three grown children, three adorable grandchildren and live in Houston, Texas. Patricia loves to hear from readers. You can write to her at P.O. Box 441603, Houston, TX 77244-1603.

Silhouette Special Edition is delighted to present

Stockwells of Texas

Available January—May 2001

***Where family secrets, scandalous pasts and
unexpected love wreak havoc on the lives of the
infamous Stockwells of Texas!***

THE TYCOON'S INSTANT DAUGHTER
Christine Rimmer
(SE #1369) on sale January 2001

SEVEN MONTHS AND COUNTING...
Myrna Temte
(SE #1375) on sale February 2001

HER UNFORGETTABLE FIANCÉ
Allison Leigh
(SE #1381) on sale March 2001

THE MILLIONAIRE AND THE MOM
Patricia Kay
(SE #1387) on sale April 2001

THE CATTLEMAN AND THE VIRGIN HEIRESS
Jackie Merritt
(SE #1393) on sale May 2001

Available at your favorite retail outlet.

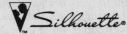

Visit Silhouette at www.eHarlequin.com

Chapter One

Rain and wind battered the casement windows of the first-floor library of the Stockwell mansion as thunder rumbled overhead. The storm had been moving toward the greater Dallas area for two days and had finally hit. But no one was complaining; the rain was a welcome change from the relentless heat and droughtlike conditions that had plagued this part of the state all summer long. Yet despite the noise of the storm, the four occupants of the room seemed oblivious to what was happening outdoors, so intent were they on their conversation.

"So we're agreed?" Jack Stockwell was saying. "I'll leave tomorrow for the Johnson farm."

Cord and Rafe, his twin brothers, both nodded.

His sister, Kate, was slower to concur, but she finally nodded, too.

As always, when regarding his sister, the hard shell Jack kept around his heart softened. He hated that her joy over her recent engagement was marred by sadness. Learning a few months back that Caine Stockwell had been lying to them all these years had shaken Kate to the core, yet her love for their father hadn't wavered, and these past few days since his death had been very difficult for her.

As it had many times since their father had confessed his duplicity, anger flooded Jack. How could Caine have done this to his children? How could he have banished their mother from their lives when they were little more than babies and then told them she was dead? Depriving them of Madelyn's presence was a despicable thing to do, and Jack wasn't sure if he would ever forgive his father. He understood his father's motives, but no matter what Caine thought Madelyn had done, he'd had no right to cut her out of their lives.

Regardless of how many times Jack told himself it was wrong, he couldn't mourn his father. Caine Stockwell had been a real bastard. From earliest childhood, Jack had known his father hated him. His feelings were evident in every word, every slap, every brutal act directed Jack's way. Caine had not once had a loving or kind word for his oldest son. Indeed, he never missed a chance to belittle Jack.

As he had so many times before, Jack wondered

what it was about him that had caused his father to hate him so much. Angry that this question continued to bother him when he should have come to terms with it long ago, he shoved it aside. What did it matter? Caine was gone. The wrongs he had perpetrated against Jack could never be changed.

"It's still hard for me to believe that Daddy didn't at least *try* to find out if Gabriel Johnson was telling the truth," Kate said, her dark blue eyes meeting Jack's. She was referring to the fact that she and her brothers had—in going through their father's papers—discovered a series of letters from Gabriel Johnson in which he accused their grandfather Stockwell of stealing Gabriel's father's fortune. He'd said he had proof and had demanded restitution. "After all," Kate continued, "the Johnsons are our mother's *family!*"

"Hell, Kate, why is it hard for you to believe? Look at what our father did to *us!*" Even though it would have given Kate some measure of comfort if they all pretended their father had been unaware of the possibility that a long-ago Stockwell really *had* cheated their mother's family out of its rightful inheritance, Jack refused to do it. First of all, he didn't believe it for an instant. Secondly, he wouldn't lie to Kate. Hell, his father didn't deserve any whitewashing of his actions. Caine Stockwell had been ruthless in his business dealings. He would not have wasted one moment of sympathy on the Johnson family, even if he thought Gabriel Johnson's claims were legitimate.

Caine's philosophy and that of his cronies echoed that of the jungle: survival of the fittest. If the Johnsons couldn't hold on to their fortune, that was their problem, not his.

And yet, even as Jack knew his father was entirely capable of turning a blind eye to any shady business deals that might have happened in 1900, as Gabriel Johnson claimed, Jack had some doubts about the authenticity of Gabriel Johnson's claims himself. If this Johnson man *really* had proof of being cheated, wouldn't he have produced it? Wouldn't he have taken Caine to court to try to get back what was rightfully his? No, something was odd about this business, and even though Jack was prepared to believe the worst about his father, he was too familiar with the way people twisted the truth to suit their own purposes to believe Gabriel Johnson's claims simply because he'd made them.

Still, if there was any possibility their ancestors really had stolen his mother's ancestors' property, the only right thing to do was make restitution. They were all agreed on that point.

In investigating, Jack had discovered Gabriel Johnson was dead, and that he'd had only two direct descendants of that original Johnson, a boy and girl who lived with their mother on a rose farm in Rose Hill, Texas.

So tomorrow Jack would leave for Rose Hill.

"What're you going to tell this Beth Johnson when you see her, Jack?"

Jack shrugged. "I'm not sure. I'm just going to nose around, see what I can find out, then play it by ear."

Cord nudged Rafe with his elbow. "See? What'd I tell you? Jack flies by the seat of his pants."

"I've been thinking on my feet for a long time now," Jack answered mildly. He was referring to the fact that he'd been a mercenary specializing in hostage negotiation and rescue missions for the past fourteen years. The only way a mercenary stayed alive was by thinking fast.

"I know," Cord replied. "I was just kidding. Rafe and I trust you to make the right decision about the Johnsons, don't we, little brother?"

Rafe rolled his eyes. Cord never missed a chance to remind him that he was eight minutes older. "Yes."

"I trust your judgment, too," Kate was quick to add.

Jack smiled at her. "Thanks. When are you leaving for Massachusetts?"

Months ago, after finding out their mother might still be alive and that there was a possibility they had a sibling they'd never known about, Jack and his brothers and sister had started trying to find them. One lead led to another, and last month Jack had gone to France to follow up on the latest information. While there he'd found a painting of a woman and a young girl who strongly resembled Jack's sister, Kate. The painting led them to a woman named Madelyn LeClaire, who lived on Cape Cod. They were fairly certain this woman and their mother were the same person, and now that their father's funeral was over, Kate planned to go back to Massachusetts to try to arrange a meeting with Mrs. LeClaire.

"On Monday." For the first time since their meeting had begun, the sadness faded from Kate's eyes. "Brett has some things he has to take care of first." Brett Larson was Kate's fiancé.

"What about you? Got any idea where you'll be staying once you get to Rose Hill?" Rafe asked, directing his question to Jack.

"No, but I'll call you once I get settled."

That decided, the four of them turned their attention to their father's will. Cord had been named executor and would work along with the family lawyer to make sure all the specific bequests were taken care of.

"You don't mind, do you, Jack?" Cord asked.

Jack shook his head. "No." Even though, by rights, as the oldest he should have been named executor of the will, he had no interest in any aspect of his father's estate. He had turned his back on the Stockwell money long ago, preferring to make his own way in the world. Besides, for once, Caine had been right to pass over Jack. Cord had been working in the family business for years. He was the logical choice to oversee distributions under the terms of the will. Rafe, a Deputy U.S. Marshal, was like Jack and had no interest in the Stockwell businesses. Nor did Kate, who was an art therapist.

With no other business to discuss, the meeting broke up and the siblings prepared to go their own ways.

"Take care," Cord said, shaking Jack's hand.

"Remember what I said about the will," Jack reminded him.

"Jack, I am not going to—"

Cutting him off, Jack said, "I don't want any of the money."

"That's ridiculous, Jack," Kate said.

"It *is* ridiculous," Rafe agreed. "You're a part of this family, just like we are."

Not just like you are.

"Jack," Kate said softly, touching his shoulder. "We can't *not* give you the money. It wouldn't be right. You're our brother."

Jack's jaw tightened. "I don't want it. I'll just give it away."

"Fine," Cord said. "If you want to give away, that's your business. My business is to follow the terms of our father's will. And he gave you an equal share of his estate."

Jack would never understand why. Caine had loved his other children, that much had always been clear. He might have lied to them, and he might have been heavy-handed in his dealings with them, especially after they became adults, but he'd loved them. So it made sense he'd leave them equal shares in his estate. *But he didn't love me.* "I don't need the money," he insisted stubbornly. "I have plenty of my own."

"So now you'll have more," Cord said.

As a negotiator, Jack knew when it was time to back down. "Fine. We'll talk more when I get back."

Kate smiled at him. "Good luck. You'll keep us posted, won't you?"

"Of course. Good luck to you, too."

"Thanks. I'm looking forward to meeting her, but I'm scared, too."

Jack nodded in understanding. Of all of them, Kate had missed having a mother the most. "Don't worry," he said softly, giving her a shoulder hug. "It's going to be okay."

Kate nodded, but she didn't seem convinced. Jack wanted to offer her more assurance, but he held back. Hell, who knew? Maybe this Madelyn LeClaire *wasn't* their mother. They were pretty certain, but they could be wrong.

A few minutes later, as he climbed the stairs to the second floor of the mansion and headed for the wing where he had a suite of rooms, Jack was still thinking about Kate's mission. She would be very disappointed if this LeClaire woman turned out not to be their mother. Worse, if she was their mother but wasn't interested in having any kind of relationship with them. He and his brothers would survive the rejection—them because they were both newly married and Jack because he was used to being rejected.

The bitter thought was one he didn't often allow to surface. And yet it was always there, waiting to pounce on him anytime he allowed himself to be vulnerable. Which was why, except for his sister, he'd always avoided close relationships. It was also why he'd chosen the profession he'd chosen, where he didn't have to depend on anyone but himself. He would be relieved to get this mystery settled, once and for all, and then head back to his solitary, answer-to-no-one life.

And if, sometimes, he was lonely, so what? Better to be lonely than to be betrayed. Telling himself he had exactly the life he wanted, he firmly pushed all other thoughts from his mind.

The following morning Jack was packed and ready to hit the road by six. The horizon was streaked with pink and gold by the time he entered the on-ramp for Interstate 20. Because it was early, traffic was light. He would make good time. According to the map, Rose Hill was fifteen miles west of Tyler, and Tyler was only ninety miles from the Dallas suburb of Grandview where the Stockwell home was located, so even stopping for breakfast, as he planned to, it shouldn't take more than a couple of hours to get there.

He debated about what approach to take, whether to head directly for the Johnson farm once he reached the area or to first see what he could find out about Beth Johnson's situation. Rose Hill was a small town, so he figured he'd have no trouble finding the rose farm. He finally decided it would be best to check in to a motel and do some investigating before going out to the Johnson place. He figured Beth Johnson must know the background of his ancestors and her husband's family. If she believed as Gabriel Johnson had believed, she probably hated all the Stockwells. Hell, if he just showed up there without warning she might shoot him on sight! Wouldn't that be ironic? he thought, chuckling aloud—to survive countless dangerous situations, to outwit passionate revolutionaries and the henchmen of despot rulers, and then to be felled by a lone woman defending her farm in Rose Hill, Texas.

When Jack reached the outskirts of Tyler, the sun was high and bright in the eastern sky and clearly illuminated how much harm yesterday's storm had caused. As he slowly drove through town, he noted the mangled trees, twisted and uprooted signs, broken windows and damaged roofs. In some places, debris blocked part of the roadway. Everywhere he looked he saw people cleaning up. It seemed the storm had been much more severe here than in Grandview. Had they had a tornado?

Less than a half hour later, a small green sign on

his right proclaimed Rose Hill, Population 297. The speed limit dropped to thirty, and Jack slowed down. He figured he'd stop at the local gas station and ask for directions to the Johnson place. But just as he made the decision, a small motel appeared ahead. It looked clean, so he swung his Dodge pickup into the driveway and climbed out. Five minutes later he was registered, paying cash in advance for one night's stay.

The owner, a garrulous old man with a shiny bald head and friendly eyes behind trifocals, handed him a key. "That there's Unit Seven," he said in a country twang. "Jest pull your truck along back and you can't miss it."

"Thanks. Maybe you can help me. I'm interested in touring a rose farm. Does anyone around here give tours?"

The old man frowned. "Mebbe. But this ain't a good time for tours. That storm did a real job yesterday. Most of the farms had lots of damage."

"What about the Johnson farm? Somebody mentioned that they have a pretty nice place."

"Used to when it was Lillian Wilder's place. But they've been havin' a rough time lately, and they had *turrible* damage from the storm. Bud Thomason up at the Sack 'n Save told me the tornado hit one of their greenhouses—the one where they do their propagatin'—and I guess all but wiped out their waterin' system. Poor Bethie was in town earlier buyin' milk for the kids. On top of ever'thin' else, her electric has been out since yestiddy afternoon. I feel so sorry for that little gal. For the past couple years, it's just been one dang thing after another.'' He tsk-tsked and shook his head, his eyes filled with sympathy. ''I don't know what she's gonna do now, what with all the cleanup and replacin' that waterin' system. See, her cousin, who *was* workin' for her, he left the beginnin' of the summer. Got him a much better job down in Houston, and I know she can't afford to hire anybody else.''

As Jack headed toward Unit Seven, he thought about what the talkative old man had told him. He couldn't help but feel sorry for Beth Johnson, but at least now he knew how to approach her.

''Mama, can we go play?'' they said in unison.

Beth wearily pushed her hair out of her eyes and straightened up, wincing at the pain that shot through her lower back. She had been working steadily since sunup, trying to salvage whatever she could from the damaged greenhouses. She'd only stopped to make a quick run into town to buy some milk for the kids' breakfast.

''Please, Mama?''

She considered her seven-year-old son and five-year-old daughter's request. They were bored. Because of the devastation the storm had caused, she hadn't wanted them out of her sight today. There were too many ways they could get hurt if they played outdoors unsupervised. Yet she felt sorry for them. After all, they were only kids.

"All right, Matthew," she finally said, "go on. But you've got to promise me you'll keep a close eye on Amy and that neither one of you will go anywhere *near* the sweet gum tree." When the tornado had struck yesterday, it had completely wiped out several trees at the back of the property, but it had only partially damaged the sweet gum, which sat on the side of the house. Now the sweet gum was unstable, and Beth was afraid it could tear loose and fall over at any time. She would have to do something about the tree, and quickly. It was a danger to her and her children as well as to the house, which had miraculously escaped any serious damage from the storm.

"But, Mama," Amy said, "our tree house is there."

"Yes, I know, sugar, but I told you earlier, you can't go up into the tree house anymore. Not until I can get somebody out here to take it from the tree."

Amy's bottom lip quivered. "But my Pooh bear is in it."

Beth sighed. "I promise you, honey, I will find a way to get your Pooh bear out of there, just not today, okay? Can you be patient a little while longer?"

Amy toed the ground with her sneaker. "Okay," she finally said.

"I'll watch her, Mama," Matthew assured her.

"All right, but I mean it, now. You must stay completely away from that tree. Do you promise?"

After giving her their solemn promises, they ran off happily. Beth watched them for a moment, then turned back to her task. Oh, God, there was so much to be done! Suddenly she felt overwhelmed, and tears blurred her eyes. Why, on top of everything else, did this storm have to happen? Wasn't it enough that Eben had left them with nothing— no insurance and no savings—and that grasshoppers had all but wiped out their plants last year?

Now this.

Yesterday's storm had caused enormous damage to the farm. One of the trees hit by the tornado had fallen on the propagation house—the greenhouse where she nurtured the cuttings taken from leftover stock and grew into viable plants. The misting system had been destroyed, and one of the tanks used to catch rainwater had been torn from the ground and thrown a hundred feet. It had missed hitting anything when it landed, which was about the only good thing Beth could say.

The other six greenhouses, which held the more mature plants—the ones she sold—had all suffered damage. Because the greenhouses weren't covered until November, the plants were sitting under open roofs. At least half of them had been completely ruined by the wind and hail. The ones remaining looked half-drowned, but Beth was hopeful they'd perk up again. If they didn't, she wouldn't have any way to obtain new root stock, because she certainly couldn't afford to buy it.

Of course, how she would tend the baby plants, even if she was able to salvage enough of the mature plants to take cuttings, she had no idea. It would have been hard enough before this happened, seeing as how she had no money to hire help, but now! A misting system was absolutely necessary, because the baby plants needed water on a regular basis. Her misting system had been automatic, turning on every hour for a few minutes. And to make matters even worse, the water used by the misting system had come from her rainwater tanks, one of which was now gone.

It seemed ludicrous. Why was she trying so desperately to hang on to the farm? Yes, it had belonged to her dear grandmother, and yes, the farm and the old country roses her grandmother had introduced to the area nearly fifty years ago were Beth's heritage and she loved them, but were they really worth the price she'd had to pay to keep them?

She thought about how she hadn't had a day off since Eben died a year ago. How she'd had to say no to Matthew when he wanted to play soccer because she knew she wouldn't be able to get him to and from practices and games. How she hadn't bought herself a new outfit in three years. How most nights they ate spaghetti or soup or meat loaf—things that didn't cost a lot of money. How her truck was ten years old and had more than 150,000 miles on it and how she prayed every day that it would last another year.

When Caleb, her cousin who had worked for her since Eben's death, left at the beginning of the summer, he'd said, "Bethie, if I were you, I'd try to sell this place."

Beth knew it would be a lot easier for everyone if she sold the farm. With the proceeds, she could buy a small house in town, get a job in Tyler, live a normal life. Yet every time she thought about leaving the roses she loved—Madame Hardy and Bloomfield Courage and Madame Alfred Carrière and Jacques Cartier and hundreds of others—she got such a desolate feeling in her stomach, she knew she would never willingly do it. Her grandmother had loved her roses passionately, and she had passed that passion on to Beth. She would never sell. Not unless she was forced to. Not unless there simply was no other way for her family to survive. *And I'm not there yet. I may be close, but there's still Grandma's jewelry.*

As she had many times since her drunken husband had run his truck into an oncoming eighteen-wheeler, she told herself it didn't matter that she was virtually penniless. That she had no idea how she would get another crop together for the spring selling period. That she had never before had to do everything herself. She was strong, and she wasn't afraid of hard work.

I have to keep this place going. This place isn't just my heritage. It's my children's heritage, too.

They were such good kids. They made up for all the bad stuff she'd had to endure during her marriage.

Beth's grandmother hadn't wanted Beth to marry Eben. "He's lazy," she'd warned. "Always wanting something for nothing." She hadn't added, *like your good-for-nothing daddy,* but Beth had known it was implied. "He'll give you nothing but grief," her grandmother had added sadly.

But Beth hadn't listened. She'd been twenty-two and a hopeless romantic. He'd been twenty-four—handsome and charming. It was a whirlwind courtship; they were married four weeks to the day after she met him at a country-western dance.

Marry in haste, repent at leisure.

Beth grimaced. Truer words were never spoken, cliché or not. Beth and Eben hadn't been married a month when he started coming home drunk. Later she found out he'd always had a problem with alcohol.

Oh, Granny, I should have listened to you. And yet, if she had, she wouldn't have Matthew and Amy today.

Beth became pregnant with Matthew almost immediately after marrying Eben. For a while after Eben found out about the coming baby, he'd tried to be a good husband, but the lure of booze was stronger than his good intentions, so when Matthew was a year old, Beth decided to leave Eben. But then her mother got sick. And her grandmother couldn't do everything—run the farm *and* take care of Beth's mother. So Beth abandoned her plan to leave Eben and talked him into moving out to the farm instead. She didn't have to do much in the way of persuading. Eben liked the idea of being a rose grower. Rose growers were respected and looked up to. That he knew nothing about growing roses didn't seem to daunt him, and to be fair, he *had* worked pretty hard that first year. Beth began to hope that he had changed.

Carrie Wilder lasted six months before succumbing to the cancer that plagued her body. A week after her funeral, Beth discovered she was pregnant again. Distraught over the loss of her mother, Beth resolved that unless things got worse, she would try to stick it out with Eben—at least until the kids were in school.

The following year, just fourteen months after her mother's death, Beth's grandmother suffered a massive heart attack and died. It was a shock to all who knew her. Lillian Wilder was only sixty-eight years old, and had always seemed indomitable.

Beth was devastated by the loss of the woman she had so admired, but there was no time to mourn. The farm was now hers. By the following week, she had taken over its management.

Eben couldn't handle it. Once again, he began to drink heavily. Beth knew his ego had suffered a fatal blow, yet how could she have done anything else? He didn't know enough about the business to run it without her supervision. So his drinking increased, and as he drank more, he worked less. Beth had to hire more help. Instead of one helper, she had to have two men, one to replace Eben, one to assist. She spent as much time as she could overseeing the work, but the children were young and needed her attention, too. She was busy day and night, too busy to worry about Eben's bruised ego.

Now he was gone and, except for the children, Beth was all alone. She wasn't beaten yet. And with that thought to sustain her, she turned back to the job at hand.

Chapter Two

Jack had no trouble finding the Johnson place. It was clearly marked with a neat white sign hanging from a rose-covered trellis.

JOHNSON NURSERY
Old Country Roses
Open Wednesday through Saturday,
10 a.m.-6 p.m.

A long gravel driveway wound through a large field surrounded by trees, gradually ending in a parking area beyond which sat a two-story redbrick and white frame house with a wraparound porch. To the right of the driveway was a garden area that contained dozens of rosebushes, interspersed with other kinds of flowers, although not many were in bloom now. Dotted around the grassy area surrounding the house were tripods and birdhouses and small trellises that were used as support structures for what Jack guessed would be called climbing rosebushes. Some of them had lots of roses in bloom, others only a few. To his left he saw half-a-dozen greenhouses, and behind the house he could see part of a barn and another greenhouse. The man at the motel hadn't exaggerated. Everything in Jack's line of sight showed storm damage, although the house and the rose garden seemed to have escaped with the least damage.

To the left of the house was a sweet gum tree that looked unstable. Several branches had been severed or partially severed and the trunk itself looked as if it had been split. As Jack drove closer, he saw that there was some kind of tree house in the sweet gum.

Somewhere out of sight he could hear a child, and down by the greenhouses, he thought he saw someone working. Looked like a woman, too. Maybe it was Beth Johnson. Turning off the ignition, he decided he would head that way.

Beth shaded her eyes and watched the unfamiliar red truck enter her property and come slowly up the road leading to the house.

She frowned. She didn't recognize the truck, but

maybe it was a customer. Pulling off her gloves, she walked toward the house.

Halfway there, she heard Matthew. His voice came from the back of the house. "Amy! Where are you?"

"I'm right here!" Amy answered.

Beth's heart knocked painfully against her rib cage as she spotted Amy, who was just emerging from the tree house, Pooh bear clutched in her arms.

"Oh, my God! Amy!" she shouted. She began to run.

Although Beth's entire concentration was focused on her daughter, who had begun to descend the tree house stairs, she was aware that a tall, dark-haired man had climbed out of the truck and, until she'd shouted, had been heading her way.

Suddenly there was a horrible cracking noise, and the sweet gum tilted to the left.

"Amy!" Beth screamed.

The stranger dashed toward Amy, reached up and snatched her off the ladder and, with Amy safely cradled in his arms, leaped out of the way just before the tree crashed to the ground. Once clear of the area, he gently set her on her feet.

"Mama!" Amy cried, racing toward Beth.

Beth nearly collapsed in relief. Tears ran down her face as she whisked her daughter—who also began to cry—up into her arms. "Oh, Amy," she said, kissing her again and again. "You scared me.

Why did you go into the tree house after I told you not to! You could have been killed.''

"I'm sorry, Mama. I just wanted my Pooh bear. He was scared up there by himself!"

Beth knew that to Amy, her Pooh bear was as real as her brother, and almost as important. "Hush, sugar. It's okay. You're okay. But don't you ever, ever, disobey me again, do you hear? No matter *what* the reason is."

"I won't," Amy said, her voice muffled as she buried her head against Beth's neck.

By now a white-faced Matthew had joined them. "I had to go to the bathroom, Mama, but she *promised* me she wouldn't move off the porch until I got back."

Normally Beth might have scolded him, but just then, she didn't have the heart to. She knew he'd been as frightened as she was. Taking a deep breath, she finally turned her attention to the heaven-sent stranger who had saved her daughter. Meeting his eyes over Amy's head, she said in a voice that still trembled a bit, "How can I ever thank you?"

He shrugged. "No thanks necessary. I'm just glad I was here." Then he put out his right hand. "Jack Stokes, ma'am."

His handshake was firm and strong. "Beth Johnson." Now that her heart was calmer, she began to assess the man who stood before her. He was very good-looking, in a rugged, Marlboro man sort of way, with a deep tan, dark thick hair cut short, and striking blue eyes. ''And these are my children,'' she added. ''Matthew and Amy.''

Matthew said a polite hello.

Jack smiled down at him and offered his hand once more.

Matthew grinned and the two shook hands.

Beth couldn't help smiling.

Amy finally raised her head. After hiccuping, she gave Jack a shy smile.

''Hello, little lady,'' he said.

''Hi,'' she said in a tiny voice.

''You probably think I'm a bad mother,'' Beth said, ''but I told them to stay away from the tree.''

He nodded.

''I'm sorry, Mama,'' Matthew said. Once again, he looked as if he were going to cry.

Beth squeezed his shoulder. ''It wasn't your fault, honey.'' It really wasn't. It was Beth's fault Amy had been in danger. No matter *how* much work Beth had to do, that was no excuse for not watching her children more closely. ''But it sure is a lucky thing for us that Mr. Stokes happened along when he did,'' Beth added, turning back toward him. Now that she in control of her emotions, and Amy was safe, she was once more curious about why the man was there.

''Well, ma'am, I didn't just happen along. I heard from Mr. Temple down at the Temple Motel that you needed some help here, and I came out to ask you for a job.''

Beth blinked. A job? He needed a job? Her gaze swept over his well-kept red pickup truck, his nice-fitting jeans, the worn but obviously well-made boots he wore, his clean hands and good haircut. Not to mention his teeth which—even though he had yet to smile—were white and straight and quite clearly teeth that had been cared for.

He sure didn't look like he needed a job. Yet he had saved Amy from possible serious injury, so for that reason alone he deserved to have his request taken at face value. ''I'm sorry,'' she said with genuine regret. ''I can't afford to hire anyone.''

''I'd work real cheap.''

Beth grimaced. ''I have to be honest. The only way I could afford you is if you'd work for free.''

He thought for a minute. ''Tell you what. If you'll give me a job, I'd be willing to work for room and board.''

Room and board? Was he serious? Why would he be willing to work for room and board? Something didn't add up.

''I'm real handy,'' he persisted. ''And I'm not afraid of hard work. I could help you get those buildings in order again.'' He gestured toward the greenhouses, then turned to the sweet gum. ''I could get that tree cleared out, too.''

It was only then Beth realized she was doubly lucky. Not only had he helped avert disaster by saving Amy, but the sweet gum had fallen away from the house.

"I'm afraid that tree house can't be salvaged, though," he said.

They both looked at the tree house, which had been demolished by the tree falling on top of it.

Amy's lower lip quivered, and Beth knew what she was thinking. Eben had built that tree house, one of the few things he'd ever made for the kids, and Amy, in particular, had loved it.

It hurt Beth to see her child suffering, but what could she say? She certainly couldn't afford to have someone build them another tree house.

Apparently taking her silence for resistance, Jack said, "I have references. I could get you some names of people you could call."

Studying him, she considered his offer. She was tempted to take him up on it, even though she was sure this man was hiding something. He had to be. No man who looked as well off as he did would need to work for room and board. "Look, I know I owe you for what you've done for me today, but you could probably go to any one of the rose farms and get work. Paid work."

"I tried the other places. They all want someone who knows something about roses." He smiled at Matthew again, and Matthew smiled back. "I don't know a thing about roses, but I wouldn't mind learning."

Oh, God, despite her doubts about him, she desperately wanted to take him up on his offer. She was exhausted, and she had so much work ahead of her if she hoped to get the farm back in working order. So what if he had something to hide? Didn't most people? And he *had* saved Amy from a terrible accident, hadn't he? Besides, he'd said he'd give her references.

"How about a trial period?" It was obvious from his tone he sensed she was weakening. "One week. If it doesn't work out, all you have to do is tell me, and I'll go."

Her eyes met his again. His blue gaze was steady and direct. Maybe she was crazy, but it also seemed honest to her. She sighed. "All right. One week."

Now he smiled. "You won't be sorry."

Maybe not, Beth thought. Then again, maybe she would. She sure didn't have a great track record when it came to judging men. Right now, though, she really didn't care. She needed help, and he was offering it. She would take her chances and hope for the best.

Jack could see Beth Johnson wasn't sure she'd done the right thing by hiring him. Hell, if he could persuade warring fanatics to release a dozen hostages, he could sure persuade one woman to let him work for her. "I could start right away." He gestured toward the tree. "If you've got a saw, I could get that tree cut up and piled over by the fence where it won't be a hazard."

She nodded slowly. ''That would be great. While you're doing that, I'll make up a bed for you on the sleeping porch. That's the screened in part at the back of the house. I hope that will be satisfactory.'' This last was said primly, and she didn't meet his eyes.

It was clear she was wary about having him inside her house. He didn't blame her. He was a stranger. For all she knew, he could be a thief or worse—a murderer. He was glad to see she was sensible as well as pretty.

For pretty she was, even though she was dressed in beat-up boots, faded blue jeans and an obviously old yellow T-shirt with dirt everywhere—on her clothes, her face, her hands, her knees. Still, no amount of dirt could disguise the fact that her slender yet womanly figure curved in all the right places, or that her strawberry-blond hair was thick and curly and shining, or that there was an appealing sprinkle of freckles on her cheeks and nose, or that her eyes were steady and clear and the warmest golden brown he'd ever seen. Yes, she was an altogether very pretty woman.

The kids were cute, too. That boy of hers looked just like her. The little girl, though, must have taken after the father, because her hair was dark and her eyes were blue. Jack hadn't been around many children in his life, but he couldn't help liking the Johnson kids. Or their mother, who was still waiting for his answer.

"The sleeping porch will be fine," he said. "But you don't have to rush to get it ready. I've paid for a night at the Temple Motel, so I might as well stay there tonight."

"Are you sure?" When he nodded, she said, "All right. But if you're going to work here this afternoon, you'll stay and have supper with us. My electricity's back on, so I can cook again." She grimaced. "Although my phone is still not working."

"On my way in I saw some telephone linemen working."

"Did you? That's good. I hope they get our service back soon."

He nodded. "I appreciate the offer of supper, but it's not necessary to feed me."

"I insist. That was the deal," she said firmly.

He could see her pride wouldn't let her accept his help today unless she could pay him something, even if it was only a meal. "Okay. Supper sounds great. Now why don't you show me where you keep your tools? I don't guess you have a chain saw?"

"As a matter of fact, I do." Leading the way to the barn, she added, "Everything you'll need is in there. While you work on the tree, I'm going inside for a bit. Matthew, you and Amy come with me."

"Ah, Mama, can't I stay out here and watch Jack?"

"His name is Mr. Stokes. You know better than

to call an adult by his first name. And, no, you may not stay out here and watch. He doesn't need you hanging around getting in the way.''

''I'd rather he call me Jack. Mr. Stokes sounds like some old man,'' Jack said, giving Matthew a conspiratorial wink.

''Can I call you Jack, too?'' piped up little Amy.

''Amy,'' Beth said admonishingly.

Jack looked at Beth. ''Mrs. Johnson, I really don't mind—''

''Beth,'' she interrupted. ''Please call me Beth. We don't stand on formalities here.''

''Beth,'' he repeated, liking the way her name felt on his tongue. ''What I was going to say is, if the kids want to watch, maybe they could sit in the bed of my truck. That way they could see, but they wouldn't be in any danger.''

''Please, Mama, please?'' Matthew begged.

''Please, Mama?'' Amy echoed.

''Oh, I guess it's all right, as long as Mr. Stokes—''

''Jack.''

She seemed taken aback by the interruption, but when she realized he'd done the same thing to her that she'd done to him, she grinned. ''Jack.''

He liked the way his name sounded on her lips, too. He also liked her smile. It was open and real, with no suggestion of anything other than genuine amusement.

''Okay, then,'' she said, ''You two can watch,

but if you get out of the truck, Jack will send you into the house, and that will be that. Understood?''

Both children nodded solemnly. ''Yes, Mama.''

After one more warning to be good, Beth left the three of them and headed for the house. Telling the children to wait, Jack went into the barn and found the chain saw. Then he and the children walked back to the truck. After getting them settled in the flatbed, Jack attacked the fallen tree.

He worked steadily for the next hour or so, and just as the kids began to get restless, Beth walked out onto the porch. Jack saw that she'd cleaned herself up and now wore fresh jeans and a light brown T-shirt.

''Time for lunch,'' she said. ''I made hot dogs.''

''Oh, boy,'' Matthew said. ''Hot dogs are my favorite.''

''They're my favorite, too.'' Amy said.

Jack smothered a smile. It was obvious Amy had a bad case of hero worship where her older brother was concerned. The way she acted reminded him of how Kate used to follow him around all the time when they were young. The twins had had each other, but Jack had always had Kate, and no matter how much their father had tried to discourage her from tagging after Jack, she had paid no attention.

''I thought we'd eat on the side porch,'' Beth said as she helped the children out of the truck.

''Cool! A picnic!'' Matthew raced around to the side porch, closely followed by Amy.

Beth shook her head. "Those two are a mess." But despite her words, it was clear she adored her children.

"They're nice kids."

"Thanks."

"Matthew's in school?"

"Yes. Second grade. And Amy's in kindergarten."

"So they didn't have school today?"

"No. It was canceled because of storm damage. I do hope they'll go back tomorrow, though. It's hard to get anything done when they're home." Her expression became rueful. "You see what very nearly happened today. What would have happened if you hadn't been here." Her eyes clouded.

Jack had an idiotic urge to put his arm around her and tell her to quit thinking about it, everything was okay now. The unexpected feeling shook him, because he wasn't normally given to emotional reactions to people. He couldn't afford them, not in his line of work.

Leaving him on the porch with the kids, she went inside. A few moments later, she returned with a laden tray containing plates and silverware, hot dogs in buns, jars of mustard and relish, a plastic squeeze bottle of ketchup, and a bowl of something that looked like macaroni salad. She set the tray down on a small metal table in the corner. The kids immediately began to help themselves.

"Wait, Amy," Beth said as Amy picked up the bottle of ketchup. "Let me help you."

"I can do it myself," Amy said. To prove her point, she turned the bottle upside down and proceeded to squirt ketchup on her hot dog. Although the amount of ketchup that ended up on the sandwich was probably twice what should have been there, Amy gave them a triumphant smile. "See?"

"You did a good job," Beth said. "Now try not to get any of that ketchup on you, okay?"

"Okay."

"Help yourself," Beth said, turning to Jack.

"I need to wash up first."

"Oh, I'm sorry. You can wash up in the barn. I don't know if you saw it or not, but in the far corner there's a little bathroom that the help—when we had help—used to use." For a moment, her voice held a trace of bitterness. Then she seemed to shake it away. "There's even a shower."

He found soap and an old but clean towel hanging from a hook next to the sink and cleaned himself up. There was a mirror over the sink, too, so he combed his hair. While standing there, he felt something against his legs and looked down. A large black cat was rubbing against his legs. "Hey, where'd you come from?"

The cat meowed, yellowish-green eyes glowing in the semidarkness of the building.

Jack leaned down and petted the cat, who arched her back and purred. He had never especially liked cats; his father had tended toward dogs—big dogs—but this cat seemed okay. Besides, it was obvious she'd taken a liking to him. It was hard to dislike an animal that liked you, he thought ruefully. She even followed him when he set off toward the house.

"I see you discovered Char," Beth said when he rejoined her and the children.

"Char?"

She grinned. "Short for Charcoal."

"She discovered me."

"Usually when strangers are here, she hides until they leave, plus she's been really spooked since the storm. She must like you."

Again he thought how much he liked Beth Johnson's smile. So far his impression of her and her children was favorable. Whether that would make a difference to his investigation, he didn't know, but he thought it probably would, because he was a pretty damn good judge of people, and Beth struck him as completely honest.

Returning her smile, he filled his plate, accepted a glass of lemonade, then sat on the top porch step and began to eat.

Beth settled the kids on the old glider that was a holdover from her grandmother's days, then decided it would be friendlier to join Jack on the steps, even though there were a couple of wooden chairs on the porch that she'd intended for them to use.

"I've been looking at your roof," he said when she was seated. "Did you know you've lost some shingles?"

Beth shrugged. "No. There are so many more immediate serious things wrong around here that I hadn't looked at the roof yet."

He nodded. "I can probably replace those shingles for you, and maybe later you can show me what else needs doing."

"Why don't we wait until tomorrow? It's probably going to take you the rest of the afternoon to dispose of that tree, don't you think?"

"Probably."

"Okay, then. Tomorrow morning we'll look at everything else."

For a while, they ate in silence, but Beth was acutely aware of his presence beside her. She was very curious about him, yet strangely reluctant to ask questions lest he think her interest something more than normal curiosity.

When they had finished their meal, she got up and went into the kitchen where she fixed a plate of cookies from a batch she'd baked a couple of days before.

"They're peanut butter," she said apologetically when she offered the plate to Jack.

"Peanut butter cookies are my favorite."

"Really? Did your mother used to bake them when you were young?"

For just a moment, something resembling pain flashed in his eyes, but it was quickly masked. "My mother left home when I was six," he said off-handedly.

Beth wasn't fooled by his attempt to be casual. Tenderhearted, she was immediately sympathetic. How awful to lose your mother when you were little more than Amy's age! And he hadn't said she'd died, he'd said she'd left home. Had she willfully abandoned him? Is that what he was saying? She was tempted to put voice to her questions, but thought better of it. Jack Stokes didn't seem like the kind of man who would share confidences easily, and certainly not with someone he barely knew. *Mind your own business,* she told herself.

But she was still wondering about him later that afternoon as she prepared supper. He was back working at the sweet gum tree. She could hear the intermittent whine of the chain saw as he cut the trunk and branches into pieces small enough to easily move.

Walking to the sink, she peered out the window. He sure didn't look like a man down on his luck, she thought again, yet what other reason could he have for offering to work for room and board? It wasn't as if Beth had anything else he might want.

She took an onion out of the wire bin hanging over the sink and, laying it on her cutting board, peeled it, then cut it into hunks. Using the food chopper her best friend Dee Ann had given her, she minced the onion, then added it to the ground meat mixture she was preparing to turn into meat loaf.

Still thinking about Jack, she rooted around in her spice cupboard for the bottle of Worcestershire sauce she was sure she had. Finding it, she sprinkled some over the meat mixture.

Could he be running from the law? Somehow he just didn't seem like the type. Besides, if he was, Rose Hill wasn't the kind of place he'd go. People running from the law usually tried to lose themselves in big cities where you could be anonymous. In little towns like Rose Hill, everybody knew everybody else's business. Beth would be willing to bet just about every one of the nearly three hundred souls who called Rose Hill home knew that a man in a red pickup truck had been hired to work out on the Johnson place. And in a day or two, they'd probably know the terms of his hiring, too. There were no secrets here.

Maybe she'd been crazy to hire him. And yet, there was something so solid and reassuring about him.

She added two eggs and bread crumbs to the meat, then washed her hands and dried them carefully. Once she was sure they were clean, she stuck them into the bowl and mixed everything by hand until all the ingredients were well blended. There was something very satisfying about mixing meat loaf by hand, she thought, remembering how her grandmother had done it the same way.

"Mama, I'm hungry."

Glancing around, Beth smiled at Amy, who had walked into the kitchen. "Supper won't be ready for a while, but you can have a banana or an apple if you want."

"Okay." Amy walked over to the table and reached into the bowl sitting in the center. Inside were two bananas and one apple. She took a banana out and began to peel it.

Beth shaped the meat mixture into a loaf. Once it was a neat oval, she placed it in the pan she'd prepared earlier. The oven was already preheated, so she stuck the meat loaf inside and turned her attention to the potatoes that needed to be peeled.

While the meat loaf baked and she prepared the mashed potatoes, green beans, and butterscotch pudding that would round out the meal, her thoughts returned to the man outside.

Maybe she *was* crazy for hiring him, but right now she really didn't care. It was comforting to have a strong, masculine body on the property, someone who could do the things she couldn't do herself, so no matter what he might be hiding, she wasn't going to look this gift horse in the mouth.

Chapter Three

"Supper's ready!

Jack looked up and saw Beth standing on the porch. The late afternoon sun had turned her hair into a fiery crown of red and gold. "Be there in a minute." He glanced down at his watch and saw it was almost six. He couldn't believe how fast the afternoon had flown by. He still wasn't finished hauling off the remains of the sweet gum tree, but he only had about an hour of work left. He should be able to finish after supper, though, if there was enough light. If not, he would come early in the morning and get it done.

Since he was finished cutting the wood, he picked up the chain saw and carried it over to the barn, replacing it where he'd found it. Then he washed up and headed for the house.

The kitchen was unlike any he'd seen before. Certainly it bore no resemblance to the massive kitchen in the Stockwell mansion, which contained the very latest stainless steel appliances and every modern kitchen contraption known to man.

This kitchen was big and square, with lots of light, but, with the exception of a fairly new looking stove, there was nothing modern about it. The top cupboards had glass-paned doors and the wood, chipped in places, was painted white. An ancient refrigerator—so old that it did not have a separate freezer compartment—stood in one corner. A quick glance revealed no dishwasher, and Jack would be willing to bet there was probably no disposal, either. The floor tile, worn and weary looking, had obviously seen better days. In the center of the room was an oval maple table surrounded by six chairs. It, too, looked ancient, its top scarred and deeply grooved from use.

Despite all this, the room was cheerful. Yellow-and-white-checked curtains on the windows, yellow paint on the walls, bright red cushions on the chairs and a red-and-yellow-flowered pillow on the maple rocking chair in the corner, along with several vases of roses and a couple of healthy-looking ferns in pots, combined to make the kitchen homey and welcoming.

The place smelled great, too, and made Jack's mouth water.

"Have a seat," Beth said with a friendly smile. Her face was flushed from cooking, which made her look even prettier than she had before. She placed a jug of iced tea on the table. The windows were open and, although there was a breeze, the room was warm. Jack wondered if the place was air-conditioned. He couldn't imagine how Beth and her kids could survive the area's sizzling hot summers if it wasn't.

"I'm sorry it's so warm in here," she said, almost as if she'd read his mind. "I'm not running the air conditioner because the compressor is making a funny noise." She made a face.

Damn, he thought. How many things could go wrong at once? "If you want me to, I can take a look at it after supper."

Her eyes brightened. "Would you?"

"Sure." Maybe the unit just needed cleaning.

Matthew and Amy were already seated on opposite sides of the table, an empty chair between them. Jack sat next to Matthew, who beamed. Beth took the chair between the two children.

"Amy, it's your turn to say grace," Beth said.

Startled, Jack bowed his head along with the other three.

"Thank you, Lord, for our food," Amy said in her sweet, little-girl voice. "And for all the blessings you give us every day."

"And thank you, Lord, for keeping Amy safe today," Beth added. "And for sending us some much-needed help."

"Amen," said Amy.

"Amen," said Beth and Matthew.

An unfamiliar emotion swept Jack. He couldn't have put a name to it. He only knew something in the simple words and their obvious sincerity had touched him deeply. He thought back, trying to remember if grace had ever been said in his home. He couldn't think of a single instance, not even on Thanksgiving. Of course, he hadn't had that many meals with his family, since his father had shipped him off to boarding school the year after his mother had supposedly drowned, and then to military school. Even during the summers, he was often away at camp or anywhere else Caine could think to send him. But even so, the times he *had* been home had been enough to show him his father cared nothing for religion, unless you counted the worship of money and power.

"Jack, do you want to start the meat loaf?"

Beth's question drew his attention back to the meal, and Jack shook off the remembrance of his lonely boyhood. He picked up the platter of meat loaf, helped himself, then passed it on.

As they ate, several things struck him. Although Jack hadn't been around many children and so didn't have much with which to compare them, he felt the Johnson kids were remarkably well behaved. They didn't argue and they didn't complain about the food. They ate enthusiastically, and when their mother spoke to them, they answered politely.

The other thing that amazed him was how comfortable he felt. These three were virtual strangers, and Jack wasn't exactly sociable, yet he felt at home. As he ate the plain but tasty food, he tried to figure out why he was at ease, finally deciding it was because Beth and her children were different from most of the people he knew. Despite their troubles, they counted their blessings, a concept unknown to most of the people Jack knew.

"Would you like more mashed potatoes?"

Jack accepted the bowl from Beth and helped himself to seconds. "The food's great."

She shrugged. "It's nothing much. Just simple country food." The pleased expression on her face belied her offhand comment.

"Well, I like it."

Now she smiled. "Good. Because it's what you're going to get from now on. Although I do promise not to serve you meat loaf more than once a week. That is," she added quickly, "if you stay."

Jack thought about their agreement of a week's trial. When he'd suggested it, he'd hoped to have his answer about the supposed swindle perpetrated by his great-grandfather before the week was up, after which he'd be on his way, but now he found himself saying, "I'll stay as long as you want me to."

After a moment, she nodded. Then, in an obvious attempt to change the subject, she turned to Matthew and said brightly, "Matthew, honey, did Mrs. Ford give you any homework?"

"Only spelling words."

"After supper we'll work on them, okay?"

"Okay."

"We didn't even think about homework last night, the storm was so bad," she explained to Jack.

"Where were you when the tornado hit? Here in the house?"

Beth grimaced. "Yes. There wasn't anywhere safer to go. We just huddled inside the hall closet and prayed."

"It was *scary!*" Amy said, eyes big as silver dollars.

"Yeah," said Matthew. "It made this big roaring sound, just like a train."

"I know. I saw a tornado once," Jack said. Then he immediately wished he hadn't, because where he'd seen it had been a small African country in the middle of a rebellion.

"You did?" Matthew asked.

"Yes, and you're right, Amy, they *are* scary."

"We were very lucky," Beth said, "even though, this morning, when I saw all the damage to the greenhouses and equipment, I wasn't thinking about being lucky. Now I'm ashamed of myself. Things can be replaced. People can't." Reaching out, she squeezed a hand of each of her children.

Although her eyes were downcast, Jack could swear he'd seen the glint of tears.

After a moment, she sighed deeply. "Well now, that's enough emotion for one day. Who wants dessert?"

"Me!" shouted Matthew.

"Me!" squealed Amy.

"Me," said Jack.

Beth grinned. "Butterscotch pudding coming right up."

The kids downed their pudding faster than Jack would have believed possible, then they politely asked if they could be excused.

"Yes, you may, but don't forget your spelling words, Matthew," Beth said. "In fact, why don't you go study them while I clean up the kitchen, then I'll go over them with you?"

"Okay."

The kids took off, and by the time Jack finished his pudding, Beth was already clearing the table. He began to help her.

"No, no," she protested, "that's not necessary. I'll do it."

"No big deal." He was used to cleaning up after himself. The way he lived, he either cleaned up after himself or it didn't get done. "If I help, the work will be finished twice as fast."

Without further discussion, they finished clearing the table together.

* * *

Beth was all too aware of him as she washed the dishes and Jack dried them. Unlike most of the men she'd known throughout her life, Jack didn't seem to feel awkward doing women's work, as Eben had disdainfully called it.

She and Eben had never shared household chores. Eben considered cooking and cleaning and doing the dishes beneath him. Not manly. Yet Beth couldn't imagine a man more masculine than Jack Stokes, and here he was, cheerfully helping her and not thinking a thing of it.

It was very pleasant working side by side. And just as Jack had promised, the work went a lot faster. Before she knew it, all the dishes had been dried and neatly stacked.

"Just show me where they go," Jack said, "and I'll put them away."

"That's okay. You've done enough." Beth removed her apron and hung it on the hook at the side of the cupboard nearest the back door, where it joined several others.

"Well, I really do want to get back outside and finish up with the tree. Plus I'll take a look at that compressor."

"The compressor can wait until morning. It's supposed to go down into the sixties tonight, so we'll be comfortable. In fact, you can finish up with the tree tomorrow, too."

"I only have about an hour's worth of work left on that tree. I'd rather get it done tonight."

"You know, as hard as you're working, you'd think I was paying you top dollar."

For a moment, his eyes met hers. Lordy, his eyes were sure blue. They reminded her of the color of the bluebonnets that covered the fields and roadsides in the spring.

"You are," he answered quietly. "You're giving me an opportunity to learn about growing roses."

For the briefest moment, his statement caused a frisson of alarm to snake through her. Was that his angle? He wanted to learn about growing roses so he could go into competition with her? But as quickly as the thought had come, it disappeared. So what if he did have some idea like that? He'd soon find out how hard this life was. Lots of people like him, who knew nothing about roses, only saw the romance of the end product. But it didn't take them long to get educated. Growing roses was just like growing corn or growing wheat or growing anything else. It was hard work. It was so hard, in fact, it would suck the life out of you if you weren't careful. A person could work seven days a week, twelve and sixteen hours at a stretch, and there would still be mountains of work left to be done. Not to mention the fact that you were constantly battling something: too much rain, too little rain, grasshoppers, a downturn in the economy. "Well, if that's what you want, that's what you'll get," she said lightly. "'Cause if I know anything, I know about growing roses."

He nodded. "Guess I'll get on out there, then."

"All right."

"When I'm done, I'll head back to the motel, but I'll be here early in the morning."

"Okay. Plan to have breakfast with us."

"You don't—"

She cut him off. "I insist. We eat at seven, because Matthew's bus comes at seven forty-five."

He reached for the handle of the screen door. "Okay. Thanks again for supper."

"You're welcome."

Almost exactly an hour later, as she sat at the kitchen table going over Matthew's spelling words with him while Amy carefully colored a picture of kittens playing with a ball of yarn, Beth heard the sound of Jack's truck starting, followed by the crunch of gravel as he turned the vehicle around and drove away down the driveway.

"Jack's leaving," Matthew said.

"Yes."

"I like him."

"I like him, too," Amy said. "He's nice."

"I wish I didn't have to go to school tomorrow," Matthew added. "Then I could help him. Can I stay home, Mama?"

"No, Matthew. It's your job to go to school and learn a lot so when you grow up you'll be able to take care of yourself."

"But you said when I grow up I'm gonna grow

roses. I can't learn about that in school.'' This last was said triumphantly.

''Yes, that's true, but in order to run a farm like this, you also have to know how to read and write. You have to know math and computers and all kinds of things.''

''Are we gonna *get* a computer?'' Matthew asked excitedly, zeroing in on the most important point just the way kids always seemed to.

''A *'puter!*'' Amy exclaimed. ''Brittany has a 'puter, and they have the Rugrats game. When I go to her house, I gets to play it.'' Brittany was her best friend Dee Ann's daughter—three years older and Amy's idol.

Beth tried to make her voice upbeat, even though it broke her heart to constantly disappoint her children. ''We can't get a computer right away, but I promise, we *will* get one.'' She'd been wanting a computer for the business, too, but it was way down on her list of priorities, because you had to have something to sell before you needed to keep records, and the way things had been going the past couple of years, all her financial resources were needed just to keep her head above water. Still…she could buy a secondhand computer for the kids. Oh, yeah, sure. If she could find a secondhand computer for sale for ten dollars, then maybe she could afford it. Fat chance.

''It's okay, Mama,'' Matthew said, reaching out to touch her hand. ''I don't need a computer.''

"Yeah," Amy said loyally. "We don't need one."

Beth swallowed against the lump in her throat. Getting up, she kissed them both in turn, saying softly, "What did I ever do to deserve two kids as wonderful as you?"

Jack got back to the motel after nine. As he drove past the office, he saw a woman inside. Mr. Temple was obviously gone for the day. Jack parked outside Unit Seven, noticing as he did that there were only two other cars in the parking lot. If that's all the business they did, he wondered how they stayed afloat. Of course, this was a weeknight. Maybe they did better on weekends, although it wasn't like this place was on a major highway. He couldn't imagine that anyone coming through Rose Hill would go anywhere else. Rose Hill would pretty much have to be your destination.

He locked his truck and walked over to his room. Just as he inserted his key into his door, a voice said, "You been gone a long time. You must have got to see some farms today."

Jack whirled around, automatically falling into a crouch and reaching for his gun. It took a moment before he realized where he was and that he had no gun. All his guns were safely locked up back at the mansion. Alarmed by his lapse, he hoped the old man—whom he belatedly realized was sitting in the shadows outside Unit Five—hadn't noticed his odd reaction.

"I didn't see you sitting there," Jack said, walking over to where the motel owner sat.

"Not many people do. That's why I like settin' here. I can see ever'thing goin' on, but nobody can see me. It's in'erestin'."

From what Jack could tell, there wasn't anything going on. *Unless you count the fact you tried to shoot Mr. Temple when he spoke to you.*

"So did you get to see some farms?" the old man repeated curiously.

"Yes, I've been out at the Johnson place." And then, because he knew the motel owner would find out about him working for Beth, anyway, Jack decided he might as well tell him. "I'm going to be working there for a while."

"Is that a fact? I guess Bethie must have scrounged up some money from somewhere, then, 'cause she was sayin' just last week how she didn't know what she was gonna do this season. I told her she could try and get a loan from the First National, but she said her granny would roll over in her grave if she mortgaged the farm. Her granny didn't believe in bein' beholden to anyone. Course, most folks in these parts feel that way, leastwise the older folks, like me. We was growin' up durin' the Depression, and we remember how so many folks lost ever'thin' to those banks, many of our parents included."

He kept on in this vein for a good ten minutes. When he wound down, Jack used the opportunity to change the subject a bit, because something had him curious. "How long has Mrs. Johnson been on her own out there? You mentioned her cousin who quit, but what about her husband?"

"That good-for-nothin'! He's long gone, and good riddance, I say. Eben died a year ago June when he had a losin' argument with an eighteen-wheeler. Drunk as a skunk, he was. Course that wasn't nothin' new. Eben, he liked the bottle more 'n just about anything."

"That's too bad."

"Yeah, folks around here, we were sure sorry for Bethie. Her granny, one of the most sensible women you'd ever meet, tried to warn her about him, but you know how young folks are. They gotta learn ever'thin' the hard way."

Now Mr. Temple was off on another tangent, which kept him going five more minutes. Jack finally managed to find a way to say good-night without seeming impolite.

"Guess I'll turn in now, too," Mr. Temple said. "It's been kinda borin' out here tonight." He got up slowly and opened the door to Unit Five.

"You live here?" Jack said.

"Yep. Ever since my wife, God rest her soul, died, I been livin' right here on the property. When Alma, that's my sister, two years older 'n me and thinks she's my keeper, asked why was I sellin' the house, I told her 'cause I wanted to, that's why, and I didn't need no other reason. That shut her up. First time in memory!'' He laughed, delighted with his own wit. Then, maybe feeling guilty about bad-mouthing his sister, he added, ''Alma, she's okay. She's got a big mouth, but she's also got a big heart.''

Later, as Jack lay in the unfamiliar, faintly uncomfortable bed and listened to the chorus of cicadas outside his window, he thought about Beth and her kids and wondered about what old man Temple had told him. Could he have exaggerated? Maybe Eben Johnson hadn't been as bad as Mr. Temple had painted him, because Beth sure didn't seem like the type of woman who would put up with that kind of behavior for very long. And she'd obviously been married to Eben awhile if Matthew was seven years old and Eben had only been dead a little over a year. Usually, if a woman stayed with a man like that, she did so because she was scared to be on her own. Weak, in other words.

Beth was not weak. Just the opposite, in fact. She was strong—a fighter, just like Jack. But fighter or not, right now she needed help. Suddenly he was very glad circumstances had sent him her way, because he was going to enjoy helping her.

Although Beth had been working hard all day and should have been exhausted enough to fall asleep as soon as her head hit the pillow, she couldn't seem to turn off her thoughts. They veered from the horrendous problems she faced in getting the farm back to working order to where she was going to get the money to make the necessary repairs to Jack Stokes and where he'd come from and why he'd ended up at her farm.

What would her grandmother have thought of him? she wondered. Somehow Beth was convinced Grandma Lillian wouldn't have hesitated. She would have hired Jack on the spot, too, the same way Beth had. Grandma Lillian had the courage of her convictions. She'd take one look at a person, size him up and make her decision. Same way with a knotty problem. She'd think about it, figure out her options, then take action. And she sure never wasted time on regrets.

"Elizabeth Lillian," she'd said more than once—she liked calling Beth by her full name since Beth had been named after her—"Once you make a decision, whether it works out or not, don't sit around crying about it. I never could abide crybabies. What's done is done. Move on."

Beth had appreciated this philosophy, especially when it became evident to everyone that her marriage to Eben was as disastrous as they'd predicted. At least she hadn't had to listen to her family say "I told you so."

Thinking about her grandmother reminded Beth again that she did have one asset left—her grandmother's jewelry. She didn't want to sell it; she wanted to keep it for Amy, but if she had to, she would. After all, jewelry was a luxury. The rose farm was their home.

A home she would be too tired to tend to tomorrow if she didn't soon get some sleep. On that thought, she punched up her pillow and determinedly closed her eyes.

Beth awakened only minutes before the alarm clock went off. The instant she tried to move, she groaned. She was so sore! Every muscle in her body ached from all the bending and stooping she'd done yesterday.

A hot shower helped and two aspirin would help even more. She studied herself in the bathroom mirror after brushing her teeth. She didn't look too bad, she thought. A little sunburned where her sunscreen had worn off, but other than that, not too much the worse for wear.

Back in her bedroom, she dressed more carefully than usual, discarding a pair of old overalls in favor of a newer, better-fitting pair of jeans and a sleeveless green cotton blouse. She took pains fixing her hair and tying it back with a green ribbon and even put on makeup, something she never did unless she was going out somewhere.

Halfway down the stairs, she stopped. What in the world did she think she was doing? She turned around with the intention of going back to the bathroom to remove the makeup. But just as she did, she heard a knock at the back door. Her heart gave a little skip. It must be Jack, she thought, flustered, and hurried downstairs to let him in.

"Good morning," he said when she unlocked the back door. His gaze swept her appreciatively.

"Good morning." Oh, God. She hoped she wasn't blushing. Her face felt uncomfortably warm. She could hardly look at him.

"I hope I'm not here too early."

"No, no, of course not." It was almost seven. "I, uh, I'm just running a little late this morning." *That's because you took so long primping!* "I—I'll have the coffee on in just a minute." Avoiding looking at him directly, she walked over to the counter where she kept her coffeemaker and turned it on. She was glad she'd had the foresight to prepare it the night before. Without turning around, she said, "I've got to go call the children. Help yourself to the coffee when it's ready." Thoroughly embarrassed and disgusted with herself for acting like a goofy teenager, she quickly made her escape.

After waking Matthew and Amy, she put out their clothes, told them not to dawdle and headed back downstairs. She found Jack standing at the window with a mug of coffee in his hands. She couldn't help noticing what broad shoulders he had and how good he looked in his snug jeans and denim work shirt. Honestly! You'd think she'd never seen an attractive man before.

"I'm making pancakes for breakfast," she said.

He turned and smiled. ''Sounds good. Anything I can do to help?''

''No, but thanks.'' Within minutes she had the pancake batter ready and the griddle heating on the stove. By the time the first batch was cooked, Matthew had clattered down the stairs and into the kitchen.

''Jack, you're here already! I didn't hear you come.'' He began to pelt Jack with questions. ''What're you and Mama gonna do today? Did you bring your stuff with you? Is it out in the truck? Are you gonna move it all out to the sleeping porch? Have you ever slept on a sleeping porch before? Are you gonna eat with us again tonight? When I get home from school, can I help you?''

''Matthew!'' Beth walked over to the table and put a plate down in front of her son. ''I'm sure Jack would like to eat his breakfast without having to answer fifty million questions. Now eat your pancakes or you'll be late for your bus.'' Her voice was sharper than she'd intended.

''It's okay,'' Jack said quietly.

Matthew gave her a bewildered look, and Beth immediately felt bad. There'd been no call for her to be so short with him. ''I'm sorry, honey.'' She squeezed his shoulder. ''I didn't mean to snap at you. It's just that I've got a headache this morning.'' Feeling like a fool, she didn't look at Jack.

By now Amy had entered the kitchen. She immediately plopped down on one of the chairs and asked Beth to tie her sneakers. Grateful for the interruption, Beth took care of the chore, and the awkward moment passed. By the time she'd served Amy and eaten a couple of pancakes herself, she had managed to regain her equilibrium.

But the morning's experience told Beth something important. Jack Stokes was far too attractive, and she was going to have to be darned careful not to make a total fool of herself during his stay.

Chapter Four

Jack did his best. He cleaned the compressor fan using a hose to blow out the accumulated dirt and leaves, then turned the air-conditioning unit back on, but the compressor was still making an alarming whining noise. He was afraid there was no hope for the equipment, which was obviously old. Beth would probably need to replace it.

He hated telling her, although he figured she probably expected it. Yesterday, when she'd told him about the problem, she'd seemed resigned to bad news. He waited until after she'd gotten Amy on the bus before saying anything.

"Oh, well." She gave him a weary smile. "At least it's heading on toward winter, so I don't have to do anything immediately."

Jack started to say there'd still be a lot of days throughout September that would be uncomfortably warm, but stopped. She knew that. Him pointing out the obvious would solve nothing. It was clear she didn't have the money to fix the air-conditioning unit. He thought about the fortune available to him and his brothers and sister. How the cost of one compressor was a drop in the ocean compared to what Beth had. If his family really *had* cheated her children out of their rightful inheritance, it was a dirty shame for Beth and her kids to suffer even one minute for lack of resources. But Jack's hands were tied. There wasn't a thing he could do about helping her financially unless he could prove she was owed the money, for if he'd learned anything in the hours since he'd met Beth, it was that she was proud. She hadn't said so, but he instinctively knew she would never take something that didn't belong to her.

"You ready for that tour?" she said.

"Sure."

"I thought we'd start with the propagation house, since it had the most damage and since it's the most important of the greenhouses."

"Okay."

Beth led the way to the greenhouse located next to the barn. From what Jack could see, it was the only one that was currently covered, although the double plastic covering had been torn loose in several places, and several of the metal bows that made up the framework were bent.

"This is where we bring the cuttings and tend them until they take root," she explained. "Once they've rooted, they can be transferred from these small containers—" she picked up a two-inch-square plastic container to show him "—to two-gallon containers and placed in a regular greenhouse."

"What's the difference between this greenhouse and a regular greenhouse?"

"This one is more carefully monitored because these plants, the ones we're coaxing into growing their own roots, are more fragile. Instead of watering by hand, which is what we do in the other greenhouses, we have a misting system here. One that's on a timer." She indicated a series of narrow pipes that crisscrossed the inside of the propagation house. At regular intervals along the pipes were small heads. "The water is sprayed out of the control heads in a fine mist," she explained. "Unfortunately, as you can see, the system was damaged in the storm." She pointed out where a couple of the pipes had been twisted, and how one section was completely gone.

"Can you still use the system?"

She shook her head. "No. It'll have to be repaired." Shrugging, she added, "we don't need it right now because the wind and hail destroyed the cuttings that were in here, so there's nothing to mist. I'm going to have to start all over by taking new cuttings. But I can't do that until I know I can care for them the way they need to be cared for.''

''So getting this place up to speed is the number-one priority.''

''Yes.'' She grimaced. ''And all it's going to take to accomplish that is blood, sweat and money.''

''I always thought greenhouses were made out of glass.''

Beth smiled. ''That's a common misconception. In northern climates, they *are* made of glass, but here in Texas, it doesn't get that cold or stay that cold for very long. Plus glass is terribly expensive. God, if I had glass to replace on all these greenhouses, I think I'd just shoot myself and be done with it!''

''What about the plastic? Does that have to be replaced?''

''Yes. But that's not a big deal. I can afford that. It's the misting system that's crucial.''

''And the metal frame?''

''We could live with that for now, as long as we get the place covered.''

''Before we talk about what else needs to be done, why don't you go over your timetable for me? What you do and when. That way I'll have a better understanding of everything.''

''All right. Let's begin with now, September. This is when we start striking—taking our cuttings from leftover stock. Once you begin striking, you're pretty much confined to the place, because as I said earlier, the cuttings have to be monitored constantly. If it's too hot in the propagation house, you have to adjust the misting system and give the plants more water. If the day is cloudy, you adjust for less water. If you don't cut back on the water, you could rot the roots, and then you'd have to throw out what you had and begin again. What you're striving for is optimum conditions for your cuttings to take root and grow.''

''How long does that take?''

''Some cuttings will root in forty-five days. Others will take as long as sixty days.''

''Let me see if I have this straight. Once a cutting roots, you transfer it to one of those two-gallon containers, then you put it out in one of the regular greenhouses. When you do that, you put a new cutting in its place, so you always have new cuttings in here.''

''Exactly.''

Jack nodded. ''Okay, I think I understand about the propagation house.''

''One other thing I forgot to tell you is that the water we use in the system is rainwater because our well water's pH is too high. Rainwater is perfect, and we catch ours in two two-thousand gallon holding tanks. However, the tornado took out our pump, which pumped the rainwater from the holding tanks to the propagation house. You might have noticed the pump laying down there by the last green-house.''

This last statement was said so matter-of-factly, it took a moment or two before Jack realized the seriousness of it.

''About November,'' Beth continued, ''we start preparing to cover the rest of the greenhouses. We buy our plastic and have it ready, and the first day there's no wind, we get the plastic up and fastened to the bows. For the rest of the winter, we concentrate on growing our plants and increasing our stock. Spring is the big selling season, when everything is in bloom. Summer is the off season, when we catch up on everything else.'' Her soft brown eyes met his. ''It's hard work, it never ends, and small growers like me don't make a lot of money.''

''Why do you do it, then?''

She sighed. ''I love this place. It's in my blood. My grandmother was a true rosarian—passionate about her roses. I grew up with that. Over the years, she taught me everything she knew. I want to pass that love on to my children. It means everything to me to make a success of this place, to keep my grandmother's heritage intact.''

Jack couldn't imagine caring about something as much as Beth cared about her farm and the roses she grew. To him, what he did for a living was just a job. Granted, his job was unusual—you didn't run into mercenaries on every corner—but he hadn't chosen it because it meant something to him. He'd chosen it to thumb his nose at his father, to say *See? You thought I was going to suffer in military school. That I'd hate it. Instead I learned something useful. Something you could never have done!*

He hadn't started out wanting to be a mercenary. He'd intended to try to get a job on an oil rig. Something blue-collar and physical. Something that would upset his father.

But then when he was in his last year of military school, he'd become friends with Tim Hastings, a boy who had been living in Europe with his family—his father was career army—and had transferred into Jack's school at the beginning of the term. His father had pulled strings to get him in. One day when the two boys were talking, Tim told Jack about his Uncle Bart, who was a mercenary. Over the Christmas holidays that year, Jack had gone home to Connecticut with Tim and met his uncle.

Jack was fascinated by the life Bart led and asked him a lot of questions. Bart was a tactician who specialized in counterterrorism. He told Jack if he were ever interested in the profession to look him up. Two years later, bored with college, Jack did, and Bart took him under his wing.

Since then Jack had developed his own specialty. He knew a lot of people looked down their noses at mercenaries, believing them all to be brutal killers who didn't care who they worked for as long as they made money. That might be true of most mercenaries, but it wasn't true of Jack. He was adamant about only working for causes he believed in. And rescuing hostages and getting refugees out of countries torn apart by war was always worthwhile.

The profession had been good to Jack. He'd made a lot of money, invested it wisely—maybe he had more of his father in him than he'd realized, he thought ruefully—and now was worth quite a bit in his own right. But no matter how successful he'd been, he'd never loved what he was doing. It was important work, yes, but in the end, it was still just a job. And, as one of the women he'd dated over the years had suggested angrily when it was clear to her he wasn't interested in commitment, it was probably his way of escaping any commitment at all.

"No loyalty to anyone, is that it, Jack?" she'd yelled at him just before she threw him out.

Now, looking at the fierce love Beth held for her farm and everything it represented, Jack couldn't help feeling envious. Sure, he had money and no one but himself to worry about, but she had something more valuable, something he would never have.

Shaking off the thought, he said, "Where do you want me to start?"

She looked around with a thoughtful expression. "Until I can figure out a way to raise the money to get the misting system fixed and that pump replaced, I guess the best thing to do is go out to the greenhouses and see how much we can salvage. That's what I was doing yesterday when you came.''

He followed her across the yard and down the path that led to the other greenhouses. These, he saw, hadn't sustained any damage to their structure, but the stock inside had been pummeled by the wind, rain and hail. ''Too bad you didn't have covers on these.''

''Wouldn't have made any difference. The hail would have punched holes in the plastic. They would have still had lots of damage.'' She walked into the first greenhouse. ''I'll show you what I was doing yesterday. I only got about half done in here.''

She showed him how to determine which plants were salvageable. ''If the roots are completely gone, put the plants over there, in that pile. If not…'' She picked up a plant that had been torn out of its container and showed him that the roots were intact. ''Then put it back into the container and gently pack the dirt around it. You may need to add some potting soil. I've got plenty in the barn. Or if you need a new container, there are some stacked over there in the corner.'' While she talked, she demonstrated. ''The other thing is, if the identifying tag is still attached to the plant, you can put it over there.'' She picked up a plant that had a white tag so he could see what she meant. ''If there's no tag, put it with that group.'' She pointed to another group of plants. ''I'll have to look at those and see if I can figure out what kind of roses they are.'' At Jack's expression, she shook her head tiredly. ''Yes, that's another problem. A lot of the tags were torn off during the storm. I can't sell plants without being able to tell the customer what they're buying.''

''Can you identify them by looking at them?''

''Sometimes. Some of the plants have clearly identifiable foliage. Bloomfield Courage is a perfect example.'' She picked up a plant to show him, and he could see the glossy, dark green foliage *was* different from many of the other plants. ''Also it helps that we group our plants together and that I know which varieties are in which greenhouse. Still, some plants are so similar to others, that if they're not blooming, I'll have to wait until they are to know for sure *what* they are.''

Beginning to realize just how mammoth the job of cleanup and restoration was going to be, Jack wondered how she could ever have thought she could do it alone. ''Do you usually have this much stock left over each season?'' he asked, picking up a plant that lay on its side and checking it the way she had done.

''It depends. What we did at the end of the season—before my cousin left—was put all the left-over stock up here in the first three greenhouses. The others are empty.''

"So you sold about half of what you had?"

"A little more than half."

"Who do you sell to?"

"Well, there are a couple of nurseries in the Dallas area that cater to a fairly affluent clientele, and they've been buying from us for about six years now. Unfortunately, even though they might buy a thousand or more plants, they want the plants delivered. This past year we had to forgo that business, because there was no one to haul the plants."

"I thought you said your cousin—"

"He couldn't be in two places at one time. I needed him here. See, my trailer can only hold about two hundred plants at a time, so at a minimum we were looking at five trips to Dallas. That's several days' worth, not counting the time to load and unload the plants. Plus when you sell in that quantity, the buyer wants a hefty discount. There's a point where it almost doesn't pay you, because you're hardly breaking even." She squinted against the morning sun. "Even before last season, I'd already made up my mind to go after retail sales. I can sell a good healthy rosebush, like this Catherine Mermet—" she pointed out a plant with strong-looking stems "—for about $12.95 retail, whereas wholesale I'm lucky to get even half that."

The more she told him, the more impressed Jack was that she had been able to manage as long as she had, for it was clear to him that she hadn't exaggerated one bit when she'd said growing roses was very hard work. And yet, just the way she handled them—the pride in her voice as she talked about them—told him how much she loved her roses.

For the next couple of hours, they worked together, moving from the first greenhouse to the second. They had gotten about a third of the way through when, with a barely suppressed groan, Beth straightened. "Let's take a break. I don't know about you, but I could use something to drink."

Jack headed for the barn, where he washed up, then he joined Beth in the kitchen where she was just mixing up a pitcher of lemonade. "It's from a frozen mix. I hope you don't mind."

They sat in the shade on the back stoop while they each drank a large glass. They didn't talk, but it was a companionable silence. When they'd drained their glasses, she said, "Want another?"

"Not right now."

"I have a jug that keeps things pretty cold. I'll pour the rest of the lemonade into it and bring it down to where we're working. That way, if you get thirsty, you can help yourself."

A bit later, as they were once more working side by side, Jack said, "Do you mind if I ask you something?"

She looked up. There was a smudge of dirt on her nose, which made her look younger and more vulnerable. "No."

"Is this place mortgaged?" Although he knew

the answer, he didn't want her to know he'd been discussing her with Mr. Temple.

"No. And it never will be. Not if I can help it."

"But wouldn't a small mortgage be the answer to your problems?"

"Maybe temporarily. But what about the next time I need money? What do I do then? Go get a bigger mortgage? No. A mortgage would just be the beginning of the end. I'm not taking any chances on losing my property to some bank."

"What if you could get a loan without mortgaging your property?"

"Actually, I tried that last year, after my husband died. You know what they did at the bank? They laughed at me. No collateral, no loan. It's that simple."

Well, Temple had been right. She was adamant on the subject. He wanted to ask her what she planned to do then, but he was wary of getting too personal. After all, this wasn't any of his business, and he sure didn't want to do or say anything that would make her suspicious of him again. Right now they were getting along well, and he wanted to keep it that way.

"You're wondering what in the world I'm going to do, aren't you?"

"Well, yeah, I was," he admitted.

She pruned a couple of dead blooms, then set the plant she'd been working on off to the side where they'd been putting the still-good stock that was labeled. "I have one last asset. My grandmother's jewelry. I thought I'd take it into Tyler and see what I can get for it."

"Where are you going to take it? A pawnshop?"

She nodded matter-of-factly, but her eyes betrayed her. She wasn't as resigned as she'd have him believe. It was going to hurt if she had to sell her grandmother's jewelry.

"You don't get much when you pawn things," he said. "Is it good jewelry?"

"It's not huge diamonds or anything, but there are some nice antique pieces."

Jack thought about Kate. Maybe he could call her. She loved antique jewelry and had some contacts in the Dallas area—dealers who might give Beth a much better price. But how would he explain a phone call of that nature? A man who was working for room and board wouldn't have contacts like that. Yet even as he told himself to mind his own business, he knew he was going to try to help her. "Listen, don't do anything immediately, okay? Let me make some phone calls first. I used to work for a guy who might know some people who can help you."

"What kind of people?"

"Dealers who buy antique jewelry. You know, go to estate sales, that kind of thing."

She gave him a suspicious look, and he knew she was wondering if she could trust him. He wanted to reassure her, but he also knew he shouldn't push.

After all, he *was* lying to her. For a good cause, maybe, but he was still here under false pretenses. And yet, he had to say *something*. "If you want, you can check out the pawnshops first. Then you'll have something to compare with."

She finally nodded. "Okay. I will."

He smiled. "Good."

The subject was dropped after that, and for the remainder of the morning they didn't talk much. A little before one, when they were almost finished with the second greenhouse, Beth stretched, rolling her neck and shoulders. "I'm going up to the house to fix us some lunch. I'll call you when it's ready."

"All right."

Fifteen minutes later, they were seated on the back porch, which was screened and pleasantly cool. "This is where you're going to be sleeping," Beth reminded him.

Jack had noticed the daybed at one end and remembered she'd said the sleeping porch was here at the back of the house. "Looks good to me."

She'd made tuna fish salad sandwiches and cut up a couple of Granny Smith apples to go with them. She'd also brought out half a dozen of the peanut butter cookies they'd eaten yesterday.

"What do you want to drink? I've got water and iced tea and milk but no sodas or anything like that. I'm going to have to go into town and buy groceries. I'm running low on everything."

"Water's fine," he said. "If you like, I can pick

up groceries for you. I was going to suggest going into town after lunch, anyway. Thought I'd check out some places, see if I can find piping to replace the damaged parts of your misting system.''

''You mean you think *you* can fix it?''

''I told you I'm real handy.''

''That would be wonderful.''

''Now don't get your hopes up, okay? I don't know if I can fix it or not, but I'm willing to give it a shot.''

''Okay.''

''So do you want me to do the grocery shopping for you while I'm there?''

''I'd love for you to do it, but I was going to have to write a check. I haven't got much cash in the house.''

''I can pay for the groceries, and you can pay me back later.''

She frowned. ''I thought you were broke.''

''I never said that.''

''Well, I guess I just assumed…''

He couldn't help smiling. ''You know what they say about assuming things, don't you?''

She made a face.

''I'm not destitute, Beth. I have a stash from my last job.'' That was true enough. She didn't need to know his stash was in the mid six figures or that for most of the day he'd been wishing he could loan her the money she needed, even if it took her twenty years to repay it. *Hell, be honest,* he told himself. *You wouldn't really care if she ever repaid it.* Admitting this sobered him. He had only known Beth for twenty-four hours, yet he was willing to do things for her that he'd never done for anyone else. He'd better be careful. It wouldn't pay to get too involved with her. It wasn't like he was going to be here for very long.

They finished their lunch and, while Beth went inside to make out her grocery list, Jack got his stuff out of the truck and put it on the sleeping porch. He then walked back to the propagation house and took a closer look at the damaged pipe in the misting system. He also checked out the timer. Seeing the unit had an option for manual control, he tested to see if that part worked. Sure enough, when he turned the system on, the heads that weren't affected by the missing pipe began to spray water.

"Good," he said aloud. Maybe once that pipe was replaced, the entire system would work again.

When he walked back to the house, Beth was waiting for him. She handed him a piece of paper. "Here's my list. I usually shop at Kroger. It's right there on the main highway as you enter the Tyler city limits. There's a Chevron station on your left, then just past it, the center where the store is."

"Okay."

"I'll be down at the greenhouses while you're gone."

"All right. See you in about an hour and a half."

* * *

After Jack left, Beth didn't go straight back to the greenhouse. Instead, she went inside and tested her phone. Relieved to hear a dial tone, she punched in the numbers for Dee Ann's salon. Dee Ann Foster had been Beth's best friend since first grade. Like Beth, Dee Ann was a single mother, but her singleness came from divorce, not widowhood.

"It's amazing how I always have enough to pay the bills now that I don't have Billy gamblin' away my profits," she'd said. The two women had often talked about how neither one of them had had very good judgment when it came to men.

"Beth!" Dee Ann exclaimed when she answered the phone. "I've been worried about y'all. I tried to call you last night but there was no answer. I almost drove out to check on you, but the kids were asleep by the time I closed up shop—Thursdays are my late night, you know—so I hated to drag them out." Dee Ann's salon was located in her garage.

"We're okay. Our phone was out until this morning sometime."

"I'm so glad you and the kids are all right. Did the storm do much damage out there?"

"Oh, Lord. You wouldn't believe how much damage it did."

"I'm so sorry, hon. I've got Janelle Walters comin' in about fifteen minutes, but I'm all ears until then."

Beth launched into a description of the damage,

which was periodically punctuated by Dee Ann's exclamations of sympathy.

"Oh, man!" she said when Beth had finished. "Life seems so unfair sometimes, doesn't it?"

Beth smiled. "Yes, but one good thing *did* happen." She went on to tell her friend about Jack's arrival and subsequent hiring.

"I just can't believe this. You're always so sensible! And now you went and hired some guy you've never seen before? And he's going to be *stayin'* out there with you?"

"Yes," Beth replied meekly.

"Beth! Hiring a stranger is crazy! Why, y'all could be murdered in your beds!"

"I know, but I really don't think—"

"Who *is* this guy, and what do you know about him?" Dee Ann demanded.

Beth had to admit she knew very little.

"I swear, I can't believe you did this. Tell you what, I'm comin' out there tomorrow after I close the shop. I need to check out this guy for myself. Oh, shoot. I can't come tomorrow. Billy's mama invited us over for dinner, and I told her we'd come early so she'd have more time with the kids." Although Dee Ann and Billy weren't on the best of terms, she thought the world of his mother, who lived in Longview, and took the kids over to see her as often as she could manage. "But I'll be out on Sunday, right after church."

Still thinking about the call as she walked down

to the greenhouse, Beth wondered what Dee Ann would have to say when she met Jack. Whatever it was, at least Beth knew she'd get Dee Ann's honest opinion. If she still thought Beth was nuts, she'd tell her so, because Dee Ann never minced words.

But Beth didn't think that's what would happen.

Because in addition to never mincing words, Dee Ann had another trait.

She'd always been a pushover for a good-looking man.

Chapter Five

When Jack was out of sight of the house, he found his cell phone and turned it on. Good. It was still charged enough to use. Accessing speed dial, he called the Stockwell mansion. When the housekeeper answered, he identified himself and asked for Kate. Luckily she was there.

"Jack!" she said when she got on the line. "I didn't expect to hear from you so soon."

Quickly he explained what had happened.

"Wait a minute. You're *working* for Beth Johnson?"

"Yes."

"I'm impressed. How'd you manage that?"

"By not telling her who I really am."

"Who'd you tell her you were?"

"Jack Stokes. Said I work odd jobs, and if she provided me room and board, I could help repair some of the storm damage."

"And she bought that?"

"She might have been suspicious at first, but she seems to have accepted me now."

"I guess I shouldn't be surprised." She chuckled. "After all, you're a handsome devil."

"I don't think she cares how I look."

"Well, if you believe that, I've got this bridge I'd like to sell you."

"C'mon, Kate, be serious."

"I *am* being serious. There isn't a woman alive who doesn't pay attention to a man's looks. What does *she* look like, by the way?"

"What she looks like isn't important."

"Ah, so she's attractive."

Deciding he would ignore her comment, he said, "She's a really nice woman. So are the kids."

"Sounds like you've made up your mind about her already."

Jack smiled. "Maybe I have."

"That's not like you, Jack. You're pretty cautious about people. In fact, I can't remember the last time you accepted someone at face value."

"Beth Johnson is different."

"I knew it. I'll bet she's beautiful. Am I right?" she teased.

"Okay, she's attractive, but I don't care about

that. Thing is, she's a nice person—a good mother and a hard worker. She's had some hard knocks, and now she's trying to hang on to this farm of hers with practically no help.''

''So you feel sorry for her.''

Jack knew his sister was just trying to understand what had motivated him to act so impulsively, and he knew he would never be able to explain his actions, especially when he wasn't sure he understood them himself.

''I guess I do.'' He wanted to say he also admired her, but maybe it would be better to just leave it at this. ''Anyway, she has some antique jewelry she wants to sell, and I was hoping you could give me the names of some people who won't cheat her.''

''Sure. No problem.'' She rattled off several names and Jack wrote down the information.

''Thanks, Kate. I owe you one.''

''Hey, anytime, big brother. So, can I call you at the Johnson place if I need you?''

''Better not. Until I can tell Beth the truth, she wouldn't understand me getting phone calls.''

''What about on your cell phone?''

''Same thing. Plus I'm not sure I can keep it charged. It would be tough to explain how someone like me needs a cell phone.''

''Jack…''

''What?''

''There's something here I don't understand. I

mean, you seem to have a good feeling about Beth Johnson, so why don't you just tell her who you are and ask her if she knows anything about the letters Gabriel Johnson sent to Daddy? Wouldn't that be easier than pretending to be someone you're not?''

''If I knew how she felt about the Stockwells, I might do it. Since I don't, I think it's best to wait. When I know her better, it'll be easier to get the information I need.''

''Well, I'm sure you know what you're doing. Or not,'' she added, laughing.

Chuckling, he said goodbye.

After hanging up, Jack called two old friends, explained what he wanted, thanked them, then wrote down their names and phone numbers for Beth. He wasn't sure if she'd follow up on references, but Jack believed in being prepared.

Now that those two things were taken care of, he searched for a public phone booth and looked in the yellow pages for a plumbing supplier. He found one, but after talking to the owner of the place, he realized he wasn't going to be able to repair the misting system on his own. The fellow recommended someone who could do the work and who wouldn't charge ''an arm and a leg'' as he put it. Jack took the name and number and thanked him.

Then he headed for Kroger where he bought everything Beth had put on her list, as well as a few extras. He wished he could think of a way to pay for most of the stuff himself, but he knew she would want the receipt. If only there was some way he could help her that didn't involve her having to sell her grandmother's jewelry. But everything he thought of, he knew she'd never agree to.

It was only after he'd loaded the groceries in his truck and was on his way back to the farm that he had an idea he thought might work. Damn. If he hadn't had so many perishables in the truck, he'd have turned around and gone back to Tyler to see if he could arrange it right now.

He decided it would be better to sleep on the idea, anyway. Who knows? Maybe he'd come up with something even better. He smiled. One way or another, he was going to find a way to help her.

Beth sat on her bed and looked at the jewelry she'd spread out over the wedding ring quilt her grandmother had given her when she'd married Eben. Picking up each piece in turn, she tried to sort the jewelry into pieces she wouldn't mind selling and those she wanted to try to hang on to.

It was difficult, though. She really didn't want to sell anything. Every piece meant something to her. She fingered a lovely ivory cameo that her grandmother used to wear around her neck on a narrow black velvet ribbon. She'd told Beth it had been a gift from her parents on her sixteenth birthday. And then there was the garnet brooch that Beth's grandfather had given her grandmother on their wedding day and that Grandma Lillian had worn to church with such pride.

Beth knew the double strand of pearls with the diamond clasp that had been handed down from her great-grandmother would probably command the best price, but oh, she couldn't part with them! They were so beautiful. Somehow she'd always pictured Amy wearing them on her wedding day.

Sighing, she touched the delicate gold filigree earrings set with amethysts that had originally belonged to Great-Aunt Lizbeth, Grandma Lillian's sister. And then there was a beautiful sapphire ring that had belonged to Beth's grandfather's family and which he had given her grandmother upon their engagement.

How could she sell any of it?

A lump formed in Beth's throat as she made her final decision. She couldn't bear to sell the pearls or the sapphire ring, so those she would keep. It would hurt to sell the other pieces, too, but right now, she really had no choice.

Jack awakened to the delicious aromas of fresh coffee and frying bacon. He had slept better than he'd imagined he would. In fact, he thought, watching as the first blush of dawn brightened the morning sky, he'd had a great night's sleep. The daybed was comfortable, the night breeze had cooled the porch nicely, and the night sounds all came from nature rather than a siren or a car engine or a loud noise to mar the tranquility. Stretching, he got out of bed and took care of the morning ritual he followed faithfully no matter where he was: fifty push-ups and fifty sit-ups. He also tried to fit in a five-mile run at least three times a week, but he figured he'd have to forgo running while he was here.

Finished with his morning exercises, he headed for the barn, where he showered—noticing Beth had put some towels out for him—and shaved and dressed in clean jeans and T-shirt. Even though it was Saturday, and Beth said she probably would spend the day working around the house and waiting on any customers who might stop by, Jack intended to work in the greenhouses. He figured he could pretty much finish up with the sorting and repotting. Then maybe on Monday he could work at general clean-up of the property. Thinking about Monday, he was reminded of his idea of how he could help Beth. He still liked it. In fact, he liked it a lot. All he needed to do was find a cooperative banker. He grimaced. Much as he didn't like doing it, he just might have to swallow his pride and invoke the Stockwell name.

That decided, he headed back to the house and those enticing breakfast aromas.

Beth had decided to take the children to church on Sunday morning. She rationalized that missing one morning of work wasn't going to make that much difference—at least not until she had the propagation house going again. So Saturday night at dinner she told Jack he was free to do whatever he wanted in the morning.

"All right. I saw some woodworking equipment in the barn. Would you mind if I used it?"

"No, not at all."

"Did it belong to your husband?"

"Yes." If the children hadn't been there, listening to every word, she would have said that, like many things Eben had decided to do, the woodworking had lasted all of a month. He'd made the tree house and then lost interest. By then, of course, it was too late to return the saws and lathes and other expensive tools. "What were you thinking of making?"

"I don't know. I just like to fool around." He looked at Matthew and Amy. "Maybe I'll make you two a new playhouse."

"A playhouse!" Matthew shouted.

"You mean like the *tree house?*" Amy squealed.

"Yes, except this house would stand on the ground, not up in a tree."

"Cool," Matthew said.

Amy's smile was so bright it almost hurt Beth to look at it.

Jack looked at her. "Is that all right with you?"

Beth hesitated.

"Oh, Mama, *pleeeeeze?*" Amy said.

"I could set it up near the propagation house.

That way, when you need to work at night or on the weekends, the kids could play close by.''

Beth's reservations were caused by the fact he was already doing so much for them, and even though she'd told herself she didn't care what his motive was, she did care. Why was he being so nice?

In her experience no one, especially a person who hardly knew her, was this nice out of the goodness of his heart. Most people who did nice things did them because they got something in return.

So even as she said yes, it was fine if Jack wanted to build the kids a playhouse, she was once again riddled with doubt and wondered if she'd made a terrible mistake in allowing Jack into their lives.

''So where is he?'' Dee Ann said the minute the kids disappeared from sight.

''That's it? No hello, how are you, good to see you?''

Dee Ann chuckled. ''I get straight to the point.''

Beth laughed. ''He's out in the barn.''

''Well, what're we waiting for? Let's go.''

''Dee Ann, please. Let's not be that obvious, okay? He'll be coming up to the house for lunch in about thirty minutes. You'll meet him then.''

Dee Ann sighed dramatically. ''Well, I guess I can wait.'' She plopped a plastic container down on the counter. ''Brought you some potato salad.''

''From Billy's mama?''

"Uh-huh. She sent so much back with me, we couldn't eat it in a month."

"Good. We'll have it for lunch."

"What else are we havin'?"

"Sloppy joes."

"Great. Brittany and Jason love 'em."

Beth smiled. "And why do you think I made them?"

"Well, hurry up and get everything ready. I'm about to bust my buttons, I'm so curious about this new employee of yours."

With Dee Ann's help, they had lunch on the table in fifteen minutes. Beth wondered how Jack would feel about eating with two women and four kids. Maybe she should give him the option of taking his food out back. "Why don't you go call the kids?" she said to Dee Ann, "and I'll go get Jack."

Jack was so engrossed in his work, he didn't hear her come into the barn, and Beth had a chance to study him for a few minutes when he was unaware of her scrutiny. Bent over the workbench, he was carefully measuring a piece of plywood. The muscles in his upper arms were sharply defined and rippled when he moved. He really was a very handsome man. Dee Ann would probably salivate over him.

Just then, he looked up. In the shadowed light of the barn, his eyes looked almost black.

Beth was suddenly tongue-tied, embarrassed because he'd caught her watching him. Clearing her throat, she said, "Lunch is ready."

He smiled. "Okay. I'll wash up, then I'll be right there."

Beth wet her lips. "Um, I hope you don't mind, but I've got some company. They're going to be eating with us."

"Hey, if you've got company, I'll just bring my lunch out here."

Because Beth knew she would feel a lot less awkward if he *did* eat outside, she said, "You don't have to do that, but if that's what you prefer, that's fine."

"Well?" Dee Ann said when Beth returned to the kitchen, "where is he?"

"Washing up. Where are the kids?"

Dee Ann grinned. "Washing up."

A few seconds later, the four children came thundering down the stairs. Jason, at eleven, was four years older than Matthew, but the two boys still enjoyed playing together, and Brittany, Dee Ann's youngest, loved being a "big sister" to Amy.

They were really cute kids, Beth thought. Like their mother, they were blue-eyed blondes. Brittany's personality was like her mother's, too, all bubbles and sass, whereas Jason was quieter and more thoughtful. He was also more sensitive—just an all-round good kid, Beth thought.

While the kids were getting themselves settled and Dee Ann was handing them sandwiches and ladling out potato salad, Jack knocked at the back screen door.

"Come on in," Beth said. "Jack, this is Dee Ann Foster, a good friend of mine, and her children, Jason and Brittany. Dee Ann, this is Jack Stokes. He's working here for a while."

Dee Ann moved forward and, giving Jack her brightest smile, stuck her hand out. "Pleased to meet you, Jack."

"Nice to meet you, too."

Beth was amused by the way Dee Ann blatantly inspected Jack.

"Jack, Jack!" Matthew called. "Come sit by me 'n Jason."

"Thanks, Matthew, but I'm going to take my lunch out to the barn," Jack said.

"Don't leave on our account," Dee Ann said.

Jack just smiled in response.

"I'll fix you a plate," Beth said. She put two sloppy joes and a big dollop of potato salad, plus a couple of dill pickles on his plate. "Help yourself to a napkin and silverware. What do you want to drink?"

"What're you having?"

"Iced tea."

"That sounds good."

"So, Jack, where are you from?" Dee Ann asked.

"Originally from the Dallas area."

"Oh? Whereabouts?"

"I was born in Grandview."

"Really? That's a pretty high-class neighborhood." Though he didn't comment, she continued. "So when did you leave Dallas?"

He smiled. "As soon as I could."

Dee Ann laughed. "Yeah, I know *that* feeling. Trouble is, Beth and I never had a chance to get out of here."

"I never wanted to leave," Beth said.

Dee Ann rolled her eyes. "Well I did. But by the time I could have, it was too late."

"Dee Ann has a successful hair salon in Rose Hill," Beth told Jack, who nodded politely.

"He doesn't want to hear about me," Dee Ann said coyly, "but I'd love to hear all about him." When Jack didn't take the bait, she said, "So where all *have* you lived?"

He shrugged. "No one specific place. I've moved around a lot."

"Have you? Doing what?"

Beth wasn't sure if she wanted to choke Dee Ann for being so persistently nosy or if she was grateful to her for asking the things Beth was curious about, too.

"This and that."

Dee Ann started to ask another question, but he turned to Beth, smiled and said, "Thanks for the food."

"You're welcome."

Giving Dee Ann another smile, he said, ''Enjoy your visit.''

The minute he was out the door, Dee Ann pulled Beth over to the counter and, muttering under her breath, said, ''Now I know why you hired him!''

''Dee Ann,'' Beth said warningly, angling her head toward the children.

''They can't hear. Besides, they're not interested in what we talk about.''

''Don't be so sure.'' Beth turned to dish up another sloppy joe. ''Do you want cheese on yours? I have some.''

''No. My hips have quite enough fat on them, thank you. And quit changing the subject.'' Dee Ann grabbed hold of Beth's upper arm to keep her from walking away.

''*Dee Ann!* You're hurting me!''

''Sorry.'' Dee Ann dropped her hand. ''But you can't deny it, Beth. He's a hunk. That's the reason you hired him.''

''It is *not!* For heaven's sake, Dee Ann, you know how much I needed help.'' Beth knew her face was red. Oh, Lord, why did she have this horrible tendency to blush? Now Dee Ann would think she was right, and she *wasn't*. The way Jack looked had nothing to do with Beth's decision to take him on.

By now all the children had stopped eating and were staring at the two of them.

Beth gave Dee Ann a warning look. "Can we talk about this later, please?"

"Okay. Sure. Fine. But it won't make a bit of difference. I know what I know." And with that, Dee Ann took the sloppy joe out of Beth's hand, put it on a plate, and started helping herself to potato salad. "Now let's eat. I'm starving."

That night, as Beth thought about the things Dee Ann had said, she could feel her face heating again. Oh, she'd like to wring Dee Ann's neck sometimes. And yet, wasn't there just a tiny bit of truth in Dee Ann's accusations? After all, if Jack had been ugly, Beth might not have been quite as willing to take a chance on him.

So just because I was swayed by eyes to die for and a great body, I put myself and my kids in a position where we could get murdered in our beds!

Okay, so she was exaggerating. She doubted Jack was a murderer. Yet…he certainly was evasive. Most people, if quizzed about their jobs, would have said what they'd done. But all he'd said was "this and that." That answer could mean anything.

Maybe he's an ex-convict.

The thought came from nowhere, but if it were true, it certainly would explain some things. Beth wondered how she could find out, even *if* she could find out.

Or maybe he was exactly what he'd said he was: a man who had drifted around, done a lot of different things to make a living, and now was exploring possibilities for the future.

Deciding he had done nothing since he'd arrived that seemed the least bit threatening—just the opposite, in fact, for he'd helped her at every turn—she decided that until he did something she didn't like, she would not worry about his presence there.

On that positive note, she finally closed her eyes and went to sleep.

On Monday Jack told Beth he had a couple of things he needed to pick up in town, so instead of taking a lunch break, he would use the time to take care of his errands. He had decided he would not try to do business with the small local bank in Rose Hill, but would instead try one of the bigger banks in Tyler. Settling on the same bank Cord used in the Dallas area for much of the Stockwell business, Jack had no trouble gaining an interview with a senior loan officer, even without an appointment. Sometimes it paid to be a Stockwell, he thought cynically.

The loan officer, a smartly dressed man in his fifties, showed Jack into his glass-enclosed office.

"Mr. Stockwell! Harry Westerman. Such a pleasure to meet you." The two shook hands, then Westerman said, "Please. Have a seat." Once Jack was seated, Westerman sat behind his desk. He smiled. "Now. What can I do for you?"

Jack explained what he wanted.

Tenting his hands, Westerman gave him a

thoughtful look. "So let me see if I understand. You want me to make a loan available to Mrs. Johnson at five percent interest. You will personally secure the loan with a deposit. And you don't want her to know you are involved. We are to simply say that the U.S. government has made these low interest loans available to rose growers who had storm damage."

"Yes."

"Do you want to put a ceiling on this loan?"

Although Jack didn't think it was necessary to restrict Beth to a certain amount of money because he knew she would take only what she felt she absolutely had to have, he knew it was only smart business to do so. "Yes. Let's say a ceiling of fifty thousand." He couldn't imagine that Beth would even want that much.

"All right. I'll tell her that's the most she can qualify for."

Business concluded, the two men shook hands again. Westerman expressed his pleasure that Jack was entrusting this matter to them and the wish that they might be of service in the future.

Although Jack had expected no less, he was still pleased by the way the meeting had gone. He couldn't wait to tell Beth what he had "learned" while he was in town.

"I just can't believe it."

"Believe it," Jack said. He had found Beth down

in greenhouse row, as he thought he would. She was retagging plants.

"You're sure they will give me the loan without collateral?"

He knew she was afraid to count on anything, and he guessed he didn't blame her. "Yes, I'm sure."

"But what if I can't repay it? What then?"

"You'll repay it. But for the sake of argument, let's say you couldn't. It wouldn't matter. The loan is backed by the government."

She sighed.

"I thought you'd be happy about this."

Her brown eyes met his. "I guess I'm just afraid to borrow money. My grandmother always told me never to be in anyone's debt."

"That's good advice, but sometimes you have to look at what's the lesser of two evils."

She chewed on her cheek and stared into space. She sighed again. Slowly she nodded. "You're right. I know you are."

Jack pulled the business card Westerman had given him out of his pocket. "This is the man to call."

For the first time since he'd returned from town, she smiled. "Thanks, Jack. This really is the answer to a prayer." The smile turned wry. "I seem to always be thanking you for something. You sure you're not my fairy godfather in disguise?"

Jack knew she was joking, but the joke bothered

him, because it hit a little too close to home. Well, soon he would find a way to talk to her about Gabriel Johnson's claims, and then he could finally tell her the truth.

Chapter Six

The loan went through without a hitch, and just three days after Jack had told Beth about the government-backed assistance, she had a hefty new balance in her checking account.

Although initially she had been hesitant about borrowing from anyone, no matter how low the interest rate, once she had the loan, she had to admit it was a lifesaver. The money enabled Beth to do so many things that needed doing—not only things strictly for the business like replacing the pump and getting the misting system fixed—but it also provided the means to buy a new compressor for the air-conditioning system and a new truck, one that wasn't held together on a wing and a prayer. Beth had debated over the truck. After all, technically the low interest loan was supposed to be used for repair, but she still felt a new truck fell within acceptable guidelines for use of the money. She also ordered a new cold frame, which would give her an additional greenhouse that could be used strictly for labeling, storage and customer service. In addition, she finally placed her order for plastic panels— something she'd been putting off until she had the money—which would then be ready when it came time to cover the greenhouses for the winter.

She also insisted that now she could pay Jack something. He protested, saying he didn't know enough about what he was doing to warrant her paying him any money. They finally agreed that he would receive a nominal sum per week, far less than an experienced rose grower would get. His week-long trial period came and went, with neither of them mentioning it. Beth didn't even think about it until it had passed, but it didn't matter. There was no question in her mind that Jack could stay as long as he wanted to.

She was actually quite impressed with how quickly he'd caught on to the things she'd shown him about growing roses.

"You're a natural," she told him one day.

He'd given her a pleased smile. "Thanks. I like the work."

Over the next few weeks, the days fell into a familiar pattern. Weekdays Beth awakened at six-thirty and by eight-thirty breakfast was over, the kitchen was cleaned up, the kids were off to school, and she and Jack were working.

On Saturdays, Darrell Drummond, a high-school boy who had been looking for some part-time work, started coming out to the farm to help Jack. That way Beth was free to concentrate her energies on the house and the kids. She even allowed herself the luxury of baking bread again, something she hadn't had the time or energy to do for more than a year. As the yeasty aroma filled the kitchen and wafted out into the yard, Beth found herself humming, something else she hadn't done in a long, long time.

Sundays were a day of rest for everyone, although in the afternoons Jack could usually be found in the barn, working on the kids' playhouse or tinkering with making trellises and tripods that Beth could sell to people who wanted a support structure for the climbing roses. All the raw materials were there, because Beth's cousin Caleb had just started experimenting with some different kinds of structures when Eben had been killed. After that, of course, there'd been no spare time for anything.

In the evenings, after supper, they fell into the routine of sitting on the side porch—Beth in her grandmother's old rocker, Jack on the top step, the two kids on either side of him. Until the light faded, Jack would whittle. He made all kinds of interesting figures for the kids: dogs, cats, squirrels, cars, airplanes, dolls.

The kids adored Jack, especially Matthew. The minute he came home from school in the afternoons, he would dog Jack's footsteps. It was abundantly clear to Beth how much Matthew had missed by not having a man around the house. He emulated everything Jack did, wanting to learn everything Jack knew. Boys need a role model, she thought sadly. So now she had one more reason to be grateful to Jack. But Jack wasn't going to be around forever. What would happen when he left? She was afraid Matthew would be terribly hurt, the same way he had been when Eben died, despite the fact that Eben hadn't been much of a father.

Still, Beth knew she couldn't isolate Matthew emotionally, simply to protect him from possible hurt. So she didn't try to keep him away from Jack, and Matthew thrived under the attention Jack gave him. Her son began to learn carpentry and woodworking skills, including how to whittle. The first time he whittled something on his own—a heart that he proudly presented to Beth—the shining pride in his eyes caused Beth's eyes to fill. Later, when she had command of her emotions, she thanked Jack.

"You don't have to thank me," he said quietly. "I enjoy doing things with Matthew. He's a great kid."

Their eyes met, and there was something, some

emotion in Jack's that Beth couldn't define, yet it left her feeling warmed, even as she told herself she was in just as much danger as her son if she allowed herself to become too attached to Jack. *He's only passing through. Don't forget that.*

One Saturday, while rummaging in the attic, Beth found her mother's old folk guitar. Seeing it brought an avalanche of memories. Her mother had been so pretty; Beth had inherited her unruly strawberry-blond hair from Carrie, although her mother had had blue eyes instead of the brown ones Beth had gotten from her unknown father.

Suddenly, as clear as if it had happened only yesterday, Beth remembered a sultry summer night long ago when she was only four or five. Her mother had been sitting on the side porch, in the same place Jack sat now. She'd been strumming her guitar and singing softly—a poignant song about love and loss. Carrie's husky contralto was filled with an aching longing that Beth had recognized on some elemental level. The memory was so clear, Beth could still feel the heat of the summer night and smell the potent fragrance of Sombreuil, the climbing tea roses her grandmother had trained to grow up the porch posts, and the background noise of the cicadas singing along with her mother, and the silvery rays of the moon that caressed her mother's beloved profile as she poured her heartache out through her music.

Beth had always known her mother was sad. She

also knew the sadness was somehow connected to the fact that Beth didn't have a daddy like the other kids did. It was only when Beth got older that she fully understood her mother's unhappiness and the cause of it. One day when she was fourteen, her grandmother had told her the story.

"It's an old story, Elizabeth Lillian," her grandmother had said. "Traveling salesman comes to little town, sweeps local beauty queen off her feet with snake oil charm, gets her pregnant, and when he finds out he's about to become a daddy, he can't hightail it out of town fast enough." Grandma Lillian had sighed and shaken her head. "Your mama, she never got over it. Some women, they're like that. There's but one man for them, and when he's gone, they can't move on. Your mama, she's still a young woman, she could still build a life for herself, but she won't." Grandma Lillian's voice got sadder, and she sighed again. "No, that's not right. She *can't*."

Beth had vowed she would never, ever, fall into the trap her mother had fallen into. And yet she had. But at least she wasn't hiding away because the man she'd chosen had let her down. And she never would.

Remembering, Beth gently dusted off the guitar, whose strings were rotted away, and brought it downstairs. When Jack saw it, he offered to take it into town and get it restrung.

Beth had shrugged, saying she didn't play.

"I do," he said.

So now in the evenings, when the light finally faded and he could no longer see to whittle, he picked up the newly strung guitar and played for them. Sometimes he sang, old songs from the sixties and seventies—"I like the old stuff," he explained—and sometimes they all sang, especially when he played the really old stuff, like "You Are My Sunshine" and "Row, Row, Row Your Boat." He even accompanied Amy who loved to sing "Alphabet Song" and "Itsy, Bitsy Spider."

Sometimes, on nights like this when Beth was filled with quiet happiness and a contentment she had never before experienced, she let herself imagine what it would be like if Jack never left. Then, afraid to examine the thought and what it said about her and her feelings too closely, she would push it away. But inevitably, inexorably, it would creep back again.

One night after the kids had gone to bed, Beth found herself going back outside to rejoin Jack on the side porch. She didn't want to lose that feeling of warmth and contentment to sleep, and she knew Jack always sat outside long after she and the children went to bed.

Holding the screen door so it wouldn't bang shut, she said softly, "I thought I'd have a glass of lemonade before turning in. Do you want one?"

He turned to look at her. The moonlight fell across his face, highlighting and emphasizing the strong planes. His eyes were hidden in the shadows. "Sure."

What are you doing, Beth? a little voice asked her as she poured the two glasses and added several ice cubes to each. She knew she was playing with fire in allowing herself to like Jack Stokes too much. It was one thing to hire him to help her, quite another to make him so much a part of her life that not only she but her children would be hurt when he left.

And yet she seemed helpless to do anything else. He was there, a magnet for all of them, offering them something irresistible.

Beth's heart was beating a little too fast as she rejoined Jack, sitting next to him on the top step. For a while, they didn't talk, just listened to the crickets and birds and, somewhere far off, the faint bark of a dog.

"Did you ever have a dog?" Beth asked after a while.

"Me, no. But there were always a lot of dogs around our place. My father was a hunter."

"Was? Is he dead?"

"Yes."

Beth waited for him to elaborate and when he didn't, she said, "I never knew my father."

He turned to look at her. "What happened? Did he die before you were born?"

"No." Quietly she told him the story.

When she'd finished, he was silent for so long

she began to feel embarrassed that she'd burdened him with her tale. But then, in a matter-of-fact voice, he said, "So we have something in common."

For a moment, Beth couldn't imagine what he meant. But then she remembered what he'd said about his mother. "I forgot. Your mother left when you were just a kid. Six, isn't that what you said?"

"Yes. But I didn't tell you the whole story. My father told us she'd died in a boating accident, but he lied."

Beth stared at him. "What really happened?" she asked softly. The lack of emotion in his voice didn't fool her one bit. He might pretend indifference, but he cared. How could he help but care?

"She ran off with my uncle—my father's brother. She was pregnant, and my father didn't believe the baby was his, so he threw her out."

Beth was appalled. Not only that his mother had gone, leaving a six-year-old behind, but that his father had lied to him about it. She didn't understand either one of his parents. They sounded like *horrible* people. She tried to imagine walking out on her children. "And you never saw her again?"

"No."

"But surely you heard from her?"

"No." In that one word, said so stiffly, was a world of unspoken sadness.

"I—I don't know what to say. I'm so sorry. That must have been terrible for you."

He shrugged. "It doesn't matter. It all happened a long time ago."

"Of course, it matters. My father abandoned my mother a long time ago, too, but..." She swallowed. She rarely talked about her feelings regarding her father. "But I've always felt the loss," she continued, gathering her courage. "There's always been this empty place in my heart." She wanted to touch him, but she knew it was best if she didn't.

"That was a terrible thing for your father to do," she added when several moments went by and Jack didn't answer.

He heaved a sigh. "I guess he thought he had a good reason."

"No," she said emphatically. "I'm sorry. There is never any excuse for lying. I can see how your father would be angry and feel betrayed if he thought your mother had cheated on him, but to lie? To say she was dead? That's awful. I've told my kids over and over again that lying is one of the worst things anyone can ever do. I detest liars. I've taught Matthew and Amy they must always tell the truth. It is especially terrible to lie to someone whom you supposedly love, someone who trusts you. Lying is such a betrayal, and it doesn't accomplish anything, because in the end, liars are always found out."

"You don't think that sometimes a lie might be justified?"

"No. Never. I don't even believe in what people

call little white lies. I realize I'm probably in the minority, but I've seen the harm lies do. I just have no tolerance for lying.''

Soon after, he got up, saying he guessed he'd turn in and telling her good-night. Beth hoped she hadn't said anything to offend him. She thought back over their conversation. Maybe it had bothered Jack when she said she thought what his father had done was terrible.

She sighed. Oh, well. It was too late now to take the words back, if indeed that's what had made him take leave of her so abruptly. And yet, was she really sorry? It *was* terrible that his father had lied to him, and maybe Jack needed to hear that from an objective third party.

Beth now saw Jack in a different light. She had always felt he was hiding something or running from something, and now she thought she knew what that something was. He was running from the past. His wandering and his nomadic existence was a way to escape caring too much about one place or one person. After all, if you didn't care, you couldn't be hurt.

And with that realization, any lingering doubt she might have had about him disappeared.

She decided that tomorrow she would be especially nice to him, maybe bake some of those peanut butter cookies he was so fond of. That decided, she headed off to bed, too.

* * *

In the end, liars are always found out.

Jack couldn't fall asleep. He kept thinking about what Beth had said. How she detested liars. How there was never an acceptable reason for telling a lie. How she didn't even believe in those polite lies people told each other to keep from hurting the other person's feelings.

And he was lying to her.

Had lied to her several times.

Would she forgive him when the truth finally came to light?

Or would she throw him off her property and tell him she never wanted to see him again?

Beth showed Jack how to take cuttings. "It's called striking," she reminded him, further explaining that they usually started striking in September and continued to strike through February. "We aim for about fifteen thousand cuttings altogether."

After striking, she would label the plant, then place it in a waiting bucket. When the bucket was full, they would carry the plants into the propagation house, get them into the liners, then put them under the misting system.

She taught him how to recognize when the plants needed more water and when they needed less. She taught him how to recognize when the plants needed to be transferred to the larger containers. And in the process of teaching him how to care for and nurture the plants, she also gave him a beginning appreciation for the roses he was tending and not just for the work itself.

She was a remarkable woman, he thought, watching her as she walked through one of the greenhouses, clipping off dead blooms as she went. The sun streaming down had burnished her hair into a golden flame, and when she bent over, her jeans accentuated the curve of her hips. Jack wondered if she had any idea how beautiful she was.

He knew it was dangerous to feel this way, but he was becoming more and more drawn to Beth. He was undeniably attracted to her, despite what he'd told his sister. Beth was everything a woman should be: strong, beautiful, earthy, generous, kind.

He had found himself telling her things he'd never told anyone. After that night, the one when he'd told her about his father, they had fallen into the habit of talking for an hour or more after the kids had gone to bed.

One night, when the subject again turned to his childhood—something that obviously fascinated Beth—he told her he hated talking about it. ''I was a really lonely kid. My father was a cold man, and he wasn't really interested in me.'' That was all Jack felt it was safe to tell her until he could be completely honest about his background.

''I guess I was really lucky,'' she said. ''Even though I never knew my father, my mother was very loving, and my grandmother was wonderful. I had a wonderful childhood. A wonderful home growing up here. I've never wanted any other.''

"You *were* lucky. If I'd had this kind of home when I was a kid, I probably never would have left it, either.''

"You said you left home after high school?''

"Yes.''

"And since then, you've never settled anywhere?''

He shook his head. "Nope.''

"But don't you *want* a home?'' she asked. "I mean, surely you don't want to drift around forever.''

He knew she couldn't relate to the kind of life she thought he'd led—wandering around the world working at odd jobs. Yet if she knew what he'd *really* been doing, would it make any difference? She would still think him strange, a person who didn't belong in her world. In fact, she would probably be completely put off by what he did. "The life suits me,'' he finally said, yet her question disturbed him.

Afterward, he kept thinking about their conversation. Had he told her the truth? Did the life still suit him? Being here with Beth and her kids had shown him another way of life. A life he had always thought was not for him. Could he have been wrong? And if he was wrong, was it too late to change?

* * *

One golden September Saturday late in the month, while they were eating breakfast, Matthew asked if they could go to the East Texas State Fair. "Jason told me yesterday that his mom is taking him and Brittany today," he said wistfully.

"She is?"

"Uh-huh. She's closin' up her shop early so they can go. Can we go, too, Mama? Please?"

"Oh, I wanna go!" Amy said.

As she had in the past, Beth started to say they really couldn't afford to spend money on things like fairs, not to mention the fact that she shouldn't leave the plants during this critical propagation time, but then her eyes met Jack's across the table.

"I'll watch the plants," he said.

"No!" Matthew said, "I want you to go, too."

"Yeah," Amy said, "I want you to go, too, Jack."

"Darrell can watch the plants for one day," Beth said, shocking herself. "We'll all go to the fair."

"In that case," Jack said, "it will be my treat."

"I can't let you do that."

"Why not? If I want to spend my money having fun with you and Matthew and Amy, then why shouldn't I?"

At ten-thirty they all piled into Jack's truck and headed for the fair, which was held on the Tyler fairgrounds. The kids were so excited they could hardly sit still. Their excitement was bittersweet to Beth, reminding her of all the things they'd missed doing since their father died and her financial position had become so tenuous.

They looked so cute, she thought. Both were dressed in new jeans and boots, another benefit of the government loan, which had enabled Beth to buy them some sorely needed new clothes. Matthew was wearing a straw cowboy hat. "This is the kind *real* cowboys wear, Mama!" he'd told her proudly the day she'd bought it for him at a local discount store. Amy, not to be outdone, had on a red cowgirl hat and matching red shirt that Brittany had outgrown and passed on.

Dee Ann was so good about giving Beth the clothes her children could no longer wear, and normally, Beth was grateful. But in the past year, just knowing they wouldn't ever have anything new or different if it wasn't for Dee Ann had made it harder for Beth to accept the hand-me-downs.

But Beth didn't want to think about that today. She didn't want to think about anything serious today. Today she just wanted to have fun, something else that had been in short supply for the past year.

Arriving at the fairgrounds, Beth directed Jack to park in the lot between Mike Carter Field and Rose Stadium. After entering the fairgrounds through the southeast entrance, they scanned the schedule and decided they would let the kids ride some of the midway rides first, then head for the food pavilion and have some lunch.

"Enough already!" Beth said after she and Jack

had taken them on the Tilt-A-Whirl three times and the Ferris wheel twice.

"I just want to ride the Tilt-a-Whirl one more time," Matthew begged.

"That's what you said last time," Jack said.

Beth laughed. "Later, Matthew, okay? Give poor Jack a break."

"Yeah, give me a break," Jack said.

Matthew rolled his eyes. "Oh, all right. But can we go get something to eat then? I'm starving."

"Me, too," said Amy.

"I'm such a bad mother," Beth said, winking at Jack, "I never feed you kids."

"Ah, Mom," Matthew said.

"What's with this 'Mom' business? You never call me Mom."

Matthew hung his head sheepishly.

"Travis called him a baby 'cause he calls you Mama," Amy said.

"Amy!" Matthew said.

"Well, it's *true*," she answered indignantly.

"I'm not a baby," he mumbled.

"Of course you're not," Beth said, stifling a smile. "And it's okay if you want to call me Mom from now on."

"Me, too," Amy said. "I'm not a baby, neither."

"Either," Beth corrected automatically.

Jack grinned.

By now they'd reached the food pavilion. After

deciding what everyone wanted, Jack got the food while Beth and the kids staked out a table. By the time they'd eaten, it was nearly one o'clock.

They spent the rest of the afternoon looking at exhibits, listening to various bands and singers, watching a magic act as well as a hypnotist and a lumberjack show. In between, the kids rode more rides, ate popcorn and cotton candy, and had a wonderful, boisterous time.

It did Beth's heart good to see them so happy. It had been a long time since she'd heard Matthew laugh in such a carefree way.

"They're having a good time, aren't they?" Jack said as the two of them watched the children fishing for prizes at one of the booths.

"Yes, and I can't thank you enough for bringing us."

He turned to her, his blue eyes warm as they met hers. "It's been my pleasure."

When he looked at her like that, Beth could almost forget that he was a here-today-gone-tomorrow kind of guy. And that would be extremely dangerous, because if she did forget, she might start to think of him as a possible permanent addition to her household.

At five o'clock, just as they were walking toward the Mayfair Building where the 4-H clubs were having an exhibit, Beth saw Dee Ann and her children. Dee Ann spied them at almost the same moment.

"Well, well, well," she said, walking up to them, "look who's here." Her smile was coy as she greeted Jack. "I didn't know you were coming here today."

"We hadn't planned to," Beth said. "Matthew talked us into it. I've been looking for you ever since we got here."

"We only came about an hour ago," Dee Ann said. "I had customers until three." She was still eyeing Jack, who had walked over to where the four kids were standing. "Been to bed with him yet?" she asked sotto voce.

"Dee Ann!" Beth could feel herself blushing. "Of course not!"

"What do you mean, of course not? Dang it, girl, what's the matter with you? Hunks like him don't come along every day."

Beth darted a look in Jack's direction to make sure he hadn't heard what they were talking about, but he was engrossed in talking to the kids. Turning back to Dee Ann, she muttered through gritted teeth, "Dee Ann, I have two children, remember? There's no way I'd go to bed with *anyone* with the kids under the same roof."

Dee Ann raised her eyebrows. "Shoot, honey, if that's the only problem, and you get the opportunity, don't pass it up. I sure wouldn't if I had the chance." She grinned. "Besides, anytime you want, I'll take the kids for the night. You just say the word."

"Please, Dee Ann, can't we talk about something else? Jack isn't interested in me, anyway."

"Oh, no? You keep tellin' yourself that, honey. I see the way he looks at you. Listen. I know men. And that gorgeous hunk is *definitely* interested in you. Why, his eyes just eat you up."

"Oh, my God," Beth moaned. She wished she could disappear. If Jack had heard even one word of what Dee Ann had been saying, Beth would die.

"It's true," Dee Ann said, "whether you want to admit it or not."

Beth decided the only way she'd get Dee Ann off the subject of Jack was to walk away from her. But for the rest of the day, Beth could not stop thinking about what her friend had said. It did no good to tell herself to put the whole thing out of her mind, that even if she didn't have the kids to think of, she would never, ever, have sex with Jack. That she simply wasn't the kind of woman who could jump into bed and have casual sex with a man, no matter how gorgeous or how nice or how appealing. For her, making love had to have meaning and be part of a committed relationship.

Like it was with Eben, huh?

Well, okay, she thought, maybe sex with Eben had become a duty and little more, but they were *married.* So no matter what Dee Ann thought, sex with Jack was out of the question. After all, he had made no secret of the fact that his stay in Rose Hill was temporary.

He'd already been there a month. One of these days he would revert to type, pack up his stuff and move on.

And then where would she be?

Chapter Seven

This was a day Jack knew he would never forget. Seeing the happiness in the children's eyes, watching Beth look younger and prettier by the hour, listening to them chatter and laugh, made his heart feel lighter than it had in years.

He felt younger, too. He tried to remember if he'd ever gone to a fair before. He couldn't remember any. His father simply wasn't the kind of man to take his kids places, although since Jack had lived away from home so much of the time, it was possible Caine had done things with Jack's siblings that Jack had not been a part of. But somehow Jack didn't think so.

It was amazing how much fun something this

simple could be. Even though some of the attractions were hokey, Jack enjoyed them anyway. Or maybe his enjoyment had more to do with Beth and the kids than with anything the fair had to offer.

He loved seeing their delight in everything, and reveled in buying the kids treats. When Beth oohed and aahed over a daisy design quilt in the crafts booth sponsored by one of the churches, he bought it for her over her protests. He knew he would never forget the smile that lit up her soft brown eyes or the way she caressed the quilt as if it were priceless diamonds.

They stayed until after the fireworks. By the time they left the fairgrounds the kids were exhausted, and they had hardly driven out of the parking lot before Amy fell asleep. No more than two minutes later, Matthew was also sleeping.

"It was such a wonderful day," Beth said with a quiet sigh. "I can't remember when I've had such a good time. Thank you for taking us."

"No need to thank me. I enjoyed it, too."

A few silent moments went by, then, surprising him, she said, "Eben never took us anywhere."

"Eben was a fool."

He knew she had turned to look at him, but he kept his eyes on the road.

"The kids love being with you, you know," she said softly.

Jack's throat tightened. *I love being with them, too. I love—* Ruthlessly he cut off the thought.

Don't go there. "They're good kids," he said gruffly.

"Yes," she whispered. "Yes, they are."

They deserve better than they've gotten, he thought, wanting to voice the thought. Wanting to ask her why she had married Eben Johnson. Wanting to ask her why she had stayed with him. But he knew he couldn't. He had no right to ask her anything. The knowledge that he was lying to her and that she would despise him when she found out settled like a heavy stone in his chest.

They didn't talk the rest of the way home. Several times Jack glanced at Beth, but each time she was pensively staring out the window, and he wondered if the mention of Eben had dampened her happiness over the day. Or was she so quiet because she'd expected Jack to say something else when she'd made her comment about the kids loving to be with him and was disappointed that he hadn't? The thought bothered him, and he wished he could explain, but how could he? He was in so deep now. The time for an easy explanation was past, and when he did finally come clean with her, he knew that no matter how he explained or tried to justify his actions, she might not ever forgive him.

He was almost grateful when he saw the turnoff for the farm, even though less than thirty minutes earlier he'd been wishing the day didn't have to end.

"I'll help you carry the kids upstairs," he said

when they pulled up in front of the house and he'd cut the ignition and they realized Matthew and Amy weren't going to wake up.

"Thanks."

He took Matthew, and she took Amy. Neither awakened. Ten minutes later, both children were undressed and tucked into bed. While upstairs, Jack looked around curiously. It was the first time he'd been in this part of Beth's house, and he took note of how nice and cozy everything looked. He couldn't help comparing Beth's home to the Stockwell mansion or the various places—he sure couldn't call them *homes*—he'd inhabited over the years. None—not the opulent Stockwell mansion, not the modern condo in Rhodesia, not the plush apartment in Argentina—compared favorably with the warm and welcoming atmosphere Beth had created. Even though her kids didn't have a father around, they were lucky, because they had a mother who had made sure their home was a place they would feel secure and loved.

As Jack followed Beth back downstairs, he tried to imagine himself growing up here, but the idea of Caine Stockwell on this farm was impossible to picture.

Back in the kitchen, Jack reluctantly said goodnight. He was back to not wanting the day to end.

Beth looked up, her eyes meeting his, and for a long moment neither moved. It was very quiet in the room. Jack could hear the hum of the refrigerator and the ticking of the wall clock and, through the screen door, the whisper of the wind in the trees and the rustle and buzz of the night creatures. Beth hadn't turned on the lights when they'd come in, so the only illumination came from the night-light on the stove and the moonlight spilling in the windows.

As he looked down into her beautiful brown eyes—eyes that reflected the same need and longing he could no longer deny—what Jack wanted most in the world was to take this woman into his arms and make love to her. But he knew he had to fight the desire, because making love to Beth now would be wrong. He was there under false pretenses, and she had made her feelings about people who didn't tell the truth abundantly clear. If and when he and Beth made love, he wanted the circumstances to be honorable, which meant there could be no falsehoods between them.

And so he did the only thing he could do. He said, "See you in the morning," walked to the door, opened it and headed for his solitary bed.

Beth felt weak with disappointment and longing as she listened to Jack's footsteps on the porch. Why hadn't he kissed her? She knew he'd wanted to. She could see the wanting in his eyes.

Trembling, she sank back against the table and told herself she should be glad he hadn't. Because even though Jack had never so much as touched her, it would have been nearly impossible to stop if he had. And there was no way they could have gone farther than a kiss, not with the kids upstairs.

But even as she told herself this, she wondered why he hadn't at least made an attempt. Had she misinterpreted his feelings? Had she told herself he wanted to kiss her simply because that's what *she* wanted to believe?

Around and around her thoughts went, and there were no satisfactory answers. Finally she roused herself, poured and drank a glass of water, shut and locked the kitchen door, then slowly made her way upstairs.

That night her dreams were filled with images of Jack and the day they'd spent together. And in her dream, he didn't walk away from her after they'd put the children to bed. Instead, he took her into his arms and his mouth and hands claimed her with thrilling dominance. She whimpered in her sleep as the Beth in her dream surrendered to her passions with no thought to consequences—something a wide-awake Beth would never be able to do.

Jack heard Beth lock the door, and he was glad, because if she'd left it open, he might not have had the willpower to stay away from her. He kept picturing her upstairs in the bedroom they'd passed— the one with the big double bed covered with the beautiful quilt. Did she wear pajamas to bed? A nightgown? He knew she wouldn't sleep naked, not with her children in the house. He imagined her body and what it would look like without the impediment of clothes, all those luscious curves, and the skin that looked so smooth. He imagined touching her everywhere, kissing her everywhere, burying his face between her breasts. What would she smell like? Taste like? Feel like?

Was she a passionate lover? Would she cry out in need and then again in ecstasy?

He tried not to think this way, because the thoughts only made him miserable and frustrated, filled with a fierce longing he couldn't assuage, but he couldn't seem to stop himself.

He knew her windows were open. Was she lying there in her bed listening to the sounds of the night the way he was? Was she reliving the day they'd spent together? Was she as restless, as filled with desire, wanting him the way he wanted her?

Beth. Her name was a whisper in his heart.

It was a very long time before he fell asleep.

The next couple of days were hard ones for Beth. She felt self-conscious around Jack, sure he knew exactly what she'd imagined had happened between them. She felt his eyes on her, and she couldn't meet them.

But by the end of the week she had managed to get past those feelings, and they were back on a comfortable footing again. By Thursday night, she'd even decided she could once more join Jack on the side porch after the kids were asleep—something she'd avoided the past couple of days.

She had just come downstairs and was packing the kids' lunches for the following day, after which she'd join Jack outside, when she heard the sound of a vehicle coming up the driveway. She walked to the front of the house and peered out the screen door. Her heart sank as she recognized Randy Biggers's black truck. Randy had been Eben's best friend, and Beth had never been able to stand him. She had been so glad when she'd heard he'd left the area. Warily she watched as he lurched out of the truck, then stumbled up the porch steps. A big man with a belly that revealed his liking for beer, he had obviously had a few too many before coming.

"Well, lookee here," he said, spying Beth and grinning. "If it ain't the pretty widow jest waitin' on old Randy. How you been, Beth? Did you miss me?"

Beth didn't smile. She also didn't open the door. "Hello, Randy."

He squinted at her through the screen door. "Ain't cha gonna invite me in?"

"What do you want?"

"Now is that any kind of nice way to greet an old friend? 'Specially one that's come all the way from El Paso to see you?"

"Is that where you've been?" The minute she asked the question, she could have kicked herself.

Who cared where he'd been? She'd just been grateful he was gone.

Now his grin turned to a leer. "So you *did* miss me. I knew you would. Well, you don't hafta be sad anymore, 'cause ol' Randy's back now, come 'specially to help you out."

"I don't need any help."

"That ain't the way I heard it."

"Well, you heard wrong."

His smile faded. Grabbing the handle of the screen door, he pulled at it, but Beth had latched it. "What's wrong with you?" he whined. "I'd 've thought you'd be grateful I was willin' to help you out. Hell, girl, don't you wanna get that money Eben's family was cheated out of by those Stockwells? Old man Stockwell died a few weeks back. I heard about it even as far away as El Paso. You musta seen it in the paper."

"Oh, now I know why you're *really* here," Beth said with disgust. "I swear, you're just like Eben. Always wanting something for nothing. Well, you can just turn around and go back where you came from, because I'm not interested."

"Whaddaya mean, you ain't interested?" he demanded. "It's y'all's money! I'm tellin' you, Beth, we kin get it. All you gotta do is go along with me and prove to those Stockwells that you're Eben's missus. I'll do the rest, and I won't charge you much, either." He winked. "I'll take part of my pay in bed, 'cause I figure about now you'll be needin' a man bad.''

"My God," Beth said through gritted teeth. She kept her voice low so she wouldn't wake the children. "You disgust me. I told you I don't want that money, and I certainly don't want *you*. I can't help it if Eben felt the world owed him a living, but I don't. And you know what? If Eben had had all the money in the world, he'd still have been a lazy, drunken bum, just like you are!"

Enraged, Randy kicked at the screen, tearing a big hole in it.

He was trying to reach in and undo the latch when suddenly Jack appeared from the side porch. He grabbed Randy's arms and twisted them behind him, causing him to yelp in pain.

Smiling grimly, Jack yanked Randy backward. Randy let loose with a string of curses and tried to get away from Jack's grip, but even though he was almost as tall as Jack and certainly outweighed him, he was no match for Jack's superior conditioning and strength. Jack didn't even have to push hard to send Randy sprawling down the steps.

"If you ever come here again," Jack said in a low, controlled voice, "if you ever even so much as *look* at Mrs. Johnson again, I will personally see to it that you die a very slow, very painful death."

"W-who the hell are *you?*" Randy sputtered from the ground.

Slowly Jack came down the steps until he was

standing over Randy, who gawked up at him. "I'll tell you who I am," Jack said in that same calm, cold, menacing voice. "I'm your worst nightmare."

"You ain't got no right to—"

Randy's words were cut off by a well-placed kick aimed at his backside.

"If you don't want more of the same, you'll get going. Now. And you'll remember what I said."

Beth was shocked. There was no doubt in her mind that Jack meant what he'd said. There was obviously no doubt in Randy's mind, either, for he scrambled to his feet and ran for his truck, cursing all the way.

Jack stayed outside until the truck's taillights disappeared.

Beth's heart was beating too fast. Would Jack really kill Randy to protect her? She abhorred violence of any kind, yet she couldn't deny that Jack's actions, the way he had so easily overpowered Randy, had thrilled her. Knowing this, she could hardly meet Jack's eyes when he came inside. When she did, what she saw in their glittering depths caused her breath to catch and her insides to turn liquid. A moment later, he crushed her to him, his mouth clamping over hers in a hard, hungry kiss that Beth returned with all the buried passion and longing she'd suppressed for years.

"Beth, Beth," he muttered against her mouth, kissing her again and again. His tongue thrust deep, and he kissed her as if he would never get enough of her.

Beth wrapped her arms around his neck and gave herself up to the emotions surging through her. All rational thought was gone. There was only Jack. His mouth, his tongue, his hard body, his hands. Beth groaned as those hands, those strong, strong hands she'd watched work and play the guitar and whittle turned their magic on her. She groaned as he cupped her bottom and pressed her close enough to feel his heat and strength. It was only when he slipped his hands under her T-shirt and unhooked her bra, then cupped her bare breasts, his thumbs stroking their rigid peaks, that she was stunned to her senses. What was she doing?

With a sob, she tore herself away. "We can't," she cried. "We can't. Th-the children are upstairs." She was shaking. "I'm sorry. I—I didn't mean to lead you on."

Jack cursed himself as reality kicked in. What in hell had he been thinking? And yet, looking at Beth, with her flushed face and her disheveled hair and her lips swollen from his kisses, he knew he would do the same thing again, if she'd let him.

But what now?

He wanted her so much he didn't know how he would stand it. And she wanted him, too. Her response to him had left no doubt of that. It was only when she'd remembered she was a mother first and a woman second that she'd pulled away.

Taking a deep breath, he called upon all the discipline and willpower he possessed. He reached out, caressing her cheek. ''I'm sorry, Beth,'' he said softly. ''It won't happen again.''

Beth could hardly hold back her tears. Oh, God, she wanted this so much. She wanted Jack so much. Her body still tingled from his kisses, still strained toward him. Her breasts actually hurt, and there was this gnawing ache deep inside her. If only the children hadn't been upstairs. If only…but the children *were* upstairs, and she was their mother. She couldn't make love with Jack, she couldn't make love with anyone who wasn't her husband, not while the children were under the same roof. Besides, she thought with regret, if she did make love with him, she'd just be setting herself up for heartbreak. Because hadn't she already figured out she wasn't the kind of woman who could have sex with a man, then forget about it?

He's not going to stay. Sooner or later, he'll take off, and all that he'll leave behind is your broken heart.

''It…it's all right,'' she finally said, smoothing down her T-shirt. She wanted to rehook her bra, but she was too embarrassed to do it in front of him. *Oh, God.* What must he be thinking? She'd been wanton in her reaction to him. He probably thought she'd led him on. Realizing this, all she wanted now was to disappear. Avoiding his eyes, she said, ''I—I'd better get back to what I was doing.'' Not waiting to see if he would follow, she headed for the kitchen and the abandoned lunches.

Jack looked at her rigid back as she resumed making the lunches and knew he had to say something, anything, to dispel the awkwardness between them and take away that expression of dismay that he knew was still on Beth's face.

"Who was that guy?" he finally asked.

Without turning around, she said, "His name is Randy Biggers. He was a friend of my husband's."

"What was he talking about?"

"You mean that money he mentioned?"

"Yes."

She shoved apples into the lunch bags and closed them before she turned around.

"I heard him say something about the Stockwell family," Jack said.

Her gaze was calm now, her emotions hidden. "Have you heard of the Stockwells?"

"Who hasn't?"

She shrugged. "It's really nothing. Just some pie-in-the-sky thing that my husband was always talking about."

"What pie in the sky?" Jack pressed. This was his opportunity to find out what she knew, and he didn't intend to let it pass.

"Oh, some harebrained thing that Eben's father and grandfather used to rant about. Supposedly, a long time ago, Eben's family was cheated out of their fortune by some Stockwell."

"Is there any chance the story might be true?"

"I don't know. Eben was always saying his grandfather Gabriel had proof, but I sure never saw any."

"Did your husband ever see it?"

"He showed me this deed one time, but that only proved they'd once owned some property, not that anyone had swindled them out of it."

"What happened to the deed?"

"I still have it. It's upstairs in my bedroom."

"Why don't you go get it? Let me take a look at it."

She stared at him for a moment. Could she *really* trust him? Maybe she was crazy, but for some reason, she did. "Okay."

While she was gone, he hurriedly combed his hair and wiped the lipstick off his mouth. When she returned, a tin box in hand, he was sitting at the kitchen table with a glass of water.

She, too, had done some repair work. Her hair had been combed, she'd redone her bra and tucked in her T-shirt, and applied new lipstick. She put the box on the table in front of him, then poured herself a glass of water, too.

"The deed is on top," she said.

Jack opened the box and removed the yellowed, frayed document. He saw at once that it was a copy of a deed, not the actual deed. It showed that fifteen thousand acres of land in Fisher County had been deeded from Nathaniel Johnson to Herman Stockwell in the late 1800s.

"See?" she said. "That shows that some long-ago Stockwell got some land from some long-ago Johnson, but it sure doesn't prove there was anything wrong with the transaction."

"No," Jack said thoughtfully. "It doesn't." He didn't know much about his father's business, but he did seem to recall that a good bit of the oil that was the genesis of the Stockwell fortune had come from their wells in Fisher County—wells that still produced a respectable amount. Still, just because they owned oil wells in Fisher County didn't prove anything, either. Those wells could be located on a completely different parcel of land than the one mentioned in this deed. "But maybe there are other papers somewhere."

"It doesn't matter," Beth said wearily. "It all happened so long ago, and there's nobody around who can prove anything one way or the other. I told Eben that, but he wouldn't listen to me. He kept saying how someday he was going to get what belonged to him."

"You know, if the story is true, it does matter, because this property would be your children's rightful inheritance."

"They don't need it. They'll have the farm. I don't want them to have too much money, anyway, because I think too much money can ruin a person.

It's much better to have to work hard for what you have. You appreciate it more.''

Jack had never admired any woman as much as he admired Beth at that moment.

''Besides,'' she continued, ''I don't want to have anything to do with the Stockwells. The one time Eben called them, they threatened him. I don't think they're nice people. You don't get to be that rich by being nice.''

Jack had no answer, because down deep he knew she was right. From what he had been told about his Stockwell ancestors, his great-grandfather had started out as a wildcatter, an appropriate profession, because from all accounts Herman Stockwell had been both wild and daring. He'd also been a notorious gambler. It wouldn't surprise Jack if he'd won the Johnson property in a poker game. Or to find out he hadn't even won it honestly, for that was another thing about Herman Stockwell. He thought cheating was just another element of the game.

Beth picked up the copy of the deed and returned it to the tin box. ''I just want to forget about all this,'' she said. ''I don't need any money from the Stockwells. In fact, I don't ever want to hear their name again. All they've ever brought my family is trouble.'' Her eyes blazed with fervency. ''Because you know what? If Eben hadn't been raised to think he was entitled to something more than he had, he might have been a different person—a decent person, someone who would have been willing to work for what he wanted. Instead of ending up a discontented drunk.''

"But, Beth, it doesn't have to be that way just because you've got some money. Think about the opportunities you'd have. You could expand. You could afford to hire the best help. And you could send the kids to good colleges where they'd learn the management skills they'd need to come back home and take over the business. With a mother like you and the values you've taught them, I don't think they'd turn out like your husband.''

Stubbornly she shook her head. "What you say may be true, Jack, but it's stupid to even think about it, because there is no proof that the Johnson family was swindled out of anything, and I don't intend to waste the rest of my life trying to figure out how to get money from those Stockwells like my husband and his family did. 'Cause you know what? I've got more important things to do.''

Chapter Eight

It was ironic, Jack thought later, that now that he knew how deserving Beth was and how right it would be to restore the Johnson family fortune—if indeed, they'd been swindled by the Stockwells— she had made it clear this was the last thing she wanted.

And since he'd found out what he'd come to find out, he knew it was time for him to leave. But he didn't want to leave. Now that he'd had a chance to be part of a different kind of life, he wanted to stay, see if there was a chance he and Beth could build a future together. But he couldn't even think about doing that until he had come clean with her. The thought was daunting. If the situation wasn't so serious, it might have amused Jack, because never before had he been so scared. Not even when he'd been in life-and-death situations.

The bottom line was, Beth wanted nothing to do with liars and she wanted nothing to do with anyone who bore the Stockwell name. She'd made that very clear. And whether he wanted to be one or not, Jack was a Stockwell. A Stockwell who had been lying to her for weeks.

Filled with deep regret, Jack knew the best thing he could do for Beth was get out of her life, and the sooner the better.

Beth tossed and turned, her thoughts in chaos. She kept remembering Jack's kisses, the way his hands felt when they touched her. Just thinking about those touches made her body ache with longing.

He'd wanted her. She knew he'd wanted her. Yet he'd said nothing when she said she couldn't go any farther with the children upstairs. She had given him plenty of time to declare himself, yet he hadn't. He'd apologized for kissing her, but that was all.

That's not all. He also said it wouldn't happen again.

Remembering, Beth burned with shame, because that's not what she'd wanted to hear.

"It's a good thing the children *were* upstairs," she muttered to herself, knowing she'd been about to make a damn fool of herself.

She recalled how, when she'd turned fourteen and had begun to show an interest in Wade Burrell, who was working for her grandmother that summer, her grandmother had sat her down and talked to her, saying, "Boys are different from girls, Elizabeth Lillian. No matter how nice they are, no matter how trustworthy and upstanding they seem, they all want the same thing. And once they get it, it's all over." She had then added darkly, "Don't be like your mama and give it away free. Make 'em pay for it with a walk down the aisle."

Beth sighed and tried to get comfortable.

She thought about what had led up to those kisses she couldn't get out of her mind. How Jack had sounded when he threatened Randy Biggers. How there'd been no doubt in her mind that Jack was capable of killing Randy.

The realization gave her goose bumps.

Just what did she really know about Jack? He'd said he had been born in Grandview and that his father was dead. Other than that, the only specific thing he'd told her was that his mother had abandoned him when he was six and his father had lied about what had happened to her.

Beth didn't know where Jack had lived since those growing up years. She didn't know if he had any brothers or sisters. She didn't know what kind of work he'd done or where he'd been educated. She'd foolishly never even followed up on those references he'd given her. Why hadn't she? She didn't know. She'd intended to call those people, but then she'd gotten the loan, and she'd forgotten all about it.

Jack was educated. That was obvious. He knew about all kinds of things, and they weren't the kinds of things you learned doing manual labor. They were the kinds of things you learned from reading and studying. She remembered how one bright night he'd pointed out different constellations of stars to Matthew: Aquarius and Capricorn and Cygnus. Another time she'd heard him explaining a mathematical term and another time, when he'd been working in the barn, she'd walked in and found him listening to classical music on an old radio he'd found.

"That's a beautiful song," she'd commented, struck by the poignancy of the music.

He'd nodded. "One of my favorites. It's from *Madame Butterfly.*"

Beth had heard of *Madame Butterfly,* but she didn't know the music, just like she didn't know about the ballet or the theater. It wasn't that she wouldn't have liked to know. It was just that she'd never had the opportunity to learn.

But Jack obviously had. And if he was educated in those ways, why had he been wandering around the world working at odd jobs? And why had he ended up here, at her farm, working for practically nothing?

Too many things about him didn't add up.

You would be crazy to trust your heart to some-one who is not what he seems. You did that once, and look what happened.

Just before she finally fell asleep, she told herself it was a good thing the farm was almost back to where it needed to be, because the sooner Jack Stokes was gone from her farm and her life, the better off she'd be.

The next day Jack avoided Beth. He said he had a lot of work to do so he wouldn't be joining them for breakfast, and took his coffee and a couple of sausage biscuits out to the propagation house to eat while he was working. Then later, after the kids were off to school, and Beth went out to the prop-agation house, he headed for the other greenhouses.

All day it was like that. Wherever she went, he went in the opposite direction. His behavior only reinforced the conclusions she'd reached the night before. Even so, she couldn't help feeling hurt. He was acting as if they were strangers, as if nothing had happened between them, as if his kisses were something she'd imagined.

Finally, at two-thirty, when Beth walked down to meet Amy's school bus, she decided she wasn't going to stick around the rest of the day. Let Jack keep checking on the plants. He was perfectly ca-pable of doing so. When Matthew came home, she was going to take the kids and go visit Dee Ann. Anything to get away.

Dee Ann took one look at Beth's face and knew something was wrong. Once the kids had gone out back to play and Dee Ann and Beth were alone in the kitchen, Dee Ann said, "Okay, spill it. What happened?"

Trying not to cry, Beth told Dee Ann everything. When she'd finished, Dee Ann sat thinking. Then, without consulting Beth, she got up, marched to the screen door and called out to the kids. "Hey, guys, how about if we have a sleepover here tonight? We'll go eat at McDonald's and we'll rent a movie. What do you say?"

"Yeah, yeah!" yelled all four kids. They were jumping up and down.

"Dee Ann!" Beth said. "I can't do that. Not today. Not after what I said last night. What will Jack think?"

Dee Ann smiled. "You know what he'll think," she said softly. "He'll think exactly what you want him to think."

Just the thought of being alone tonight, of indulging her fantasies, of letting Jack make love to her, was enough to turn Beth's knees to water. "I can't."

"Of course you can."

Beth shook her head. "It's not that I don't want to. I—I'm just afraid."

Dee Ann rolled her eyes. "Oh, good grief. He's just a man, for heaven's sake."

"I don't want to be hurt."

"There's only one way to keep from being hurt, Beth. That's to stop living. Is that what you want?"

A long moment passed. Finally Beth said, "The kids don't have their pajamas or clothes for tomorrow."

Dee Ann grinned. "If that's our only problem, we can sure fix that. We'll all go back to your place right now and get their stuff."

"But—"

"Don't argue with me, Beth," she said sternly. "You know this is something you need to do. How will you ever know if you want this guy or not? Now let's go. I'll bring the kids home about noon tomorrow."

There was a twisted kind of logic to Dee Ann's argument, Beth thought. So even though she knew this wasn't wise, that she'd be oh, so much better off if she stuck to her guns and kept Jack at a distance until he was safely gone from her life, she also knew she wasn't going to be wise or safe. She was going to follow her heart, do what she wanted to do instead of what she thought she ought to do, and see where that road led.

And if, in the process, she got her heart broken, well, at least she would have *lived,* at least she would have *felt,* at least she would have taken a chance.

Certainly she didn't want her only experience or knowledge of love to begin and end with Eben. She wet her lips. Stared at Dee Ann. Then she nodded.

Dee Ann punched the air with her right fist. "All *right!*"

"Guess what, Jack," Amy called, running over to the barn where he was working. "Me and Matthew are goin' to have a sleepover at Jason and Brittany's house! We're goin' to McDonald's and we're rentin' a movie and everything!"

Jack looked up. He saw Beth and her friend walking into the house. Beth didn't look his way. "A sleepover, huh?"

"Yeah! It's gonna be so *fun!*" Amy was practically dancing up and down, she was so excited. The other kids—Matthew and the Foster woman's two—called to Amy. "I gotta go," she said breathlessly.

"Well," Jack said, "have a good time."

After she'd run off to join her friends, Jack returned to the tripod he was building, but his mind was racing. So the children would be gone tonight and he and Beth would be alone on the farm. Was there a special reason why Beth was allowing Matthew and Amy to stay at her friend's house? Was this her way of telling him she wanted them to be together tonight?

Excitement skidded through him, and all his good intentions disappeared, because Jack knew, if Beth gave him any sign that this *was* what she wanted, he would not be able to resist.

After Dee Ann and the children left, Beth was a wreck. She was afraid of what Jack might be thinking. What if he didn't want to be with her tonight?

Well, she would soon know, because in another hour, it would be time for supper. Realizing she hadn't much time, she hurriedly took out the chicken she'd thawed earlier. After dipping it into an egg-and-water mixture, she coated it with seasoned bread crumbs and popped it into the oven to bake. Then she raced upstairs and took the fastest shower she'd ever taken. She even managed to wash and dry her hair, put on a clean pair of jeans and a fresh blouse, and get back downstairs while the chicken still had twenty minutes left to bake.

In the time left, she put rice on to cook, sliced tomatoes and cucumbers for a salad, and mixed up biscuit dough. When the bell dinged for the chicken, she removed that pan from the oven and replaced it with the cookie sheet of biscuits.

When all the food was ready, she took a deep breath, willed herself to settle down, then walked out to the back porch and called to Jack. A few seconds later, he appeared in the doorway of the barn. Shielding his eyes from the afternoon sun, he said he'd be there in a few minutes.

Beth's heart thumped crazily. She was so nervous she wasn't sure she could do this. What if Jack didn't want her? What if all he did was come inside and eat and help clean up the kitchen the way he did every night? If that happened, she didn't know what she'd do. Somehow, she guessed, she would hide her disappointment, but she knew his rejection would devastate her, for now that she'd decided on this course of action, she wanted him so badly it hurt.

He took a bit longer than the few minutes he'd said. Twice Beth walked to the window and looked in the direction of the barn, but she didn't see him. What was he doing? She couldn't stand this waiting. Even if he was going to reject her, she'd rather get it over with.

Finally she saw him emerge from the barn. Scurrying back to the stove—she'd *die* if he suspected she'd been watching for him—she stirred the gravy she'd made and took deep breaths to try once again to calm herself down. She didn't turn around until she heard his step on the porch.

When he opened the screen door and walked into the kitchen, Beth saw why it had taken him so long to respond to her summons. His hair was wet, and he had changed into clean clothes. He'd had a shower!

Now Beth's heart thumped harder, and it took all her willpower to meet his eyes.

For one long, silent moment, their gazes locked.

And then, in a moment Beth knew she would never forget, he walked over to her, took the wooden spoon out of her hand and put it back into the gravy pot, and pulled her into his arms.

Making love to Beth was everything—and more—that Jack had imagined. She was incredible. Her skin was like satin, but warm and firm and fragrant. His hands trembled as he stroked her. He couldn't believe how lucky he was, that this wonderful, beautiful woman wanted him, that he was actually here, in her bed.

At first, they had kissed with greedy abandon and torn at each other's clothes. But once they managed to rid themselves of all the impediments between them, Jack forced himself to slow down.

"You're so beautiful," he whispered, trailing kisses over her collarbone, her breasts, her belly.

"I'm not."

"Yes, you are. You're the most beautiful woman I've ever seen."

She laughed softly, her breath catching as his mouth moved lower. "You…you must not have seen many women, then," she said breathlessly.

Over the years, Jack had made love to many women, but he'd never felt the way he felt now. He wanted to give Beth pleasure, more pleasure than she'd ever had before. So even though he was burning with desire and wanted nothing more than to plunge himself into her softness, he wanted to make sure she was as ready as he was.

He took his time. He explored her with his hands and his mouth, reveling each time she made that little soft sound in her throat. And in the process of pleasuring her he found that his own pleasure was intensified, that he loved knowing he was responsible for the abandonment with which she opened herself to him.

Beth had never known lovemaking between a man and woman could be like this. When she and Eben had made love, it had always been fast, because Eben could never wait. When she was younger, she hadn't realized he was a selfish lover, that as long as he was satisfied, that was all that was important to him. He hadn't even known that most of the time Beth was frustrated and unfulfilled.

Jack, though, Jack was different. He was wonderful. He seemed to know instinctively just what would bring her the greatest possible pleasure. He knew exactly where and how to touch her, where and how to kiss her. His meticulous attention to her body, the way his fingers skimmed over her skin, caused the most exquisite sensations.

She kept trying to touch him, too, but he kept gently pushing her hands away, and she finally understood that if she were to touch him, he would lose control, and he didn't want to. Not yet.

And when he finally let her touch him and hold him, when he finally raised himself over her and slowly entered her, it was better than Beth had ever imagined it could be. She wrapped her legs around him and drew him in as deeply as she could, and when he slowly began to move, she matched her movements to his.

Their shared climax, when it came, was shattering. It went on and on, so cataclysmic that Beth cried out and so did Jack.

Afterward, once their breathing slowed and their bodies calmed, Jack drew her into his arms spoon fashion. For a long while, they just lay together, not talking, not moving. Then slowly, lips against her neck, his hands began to explore her body again.

It was midnight before they decided they'd better get up and see about the mess in the kitchen.

"Anyway, I'm hungry," Jack said. He chuckled and patted her bottom. "Making love to an insatiable woman takes a lot of energy."

"Insatiable!" Beth said. She knew she was blushing, but at least it was too dark for him to see it.

His voice dropped to a husky murmur as, with his forefinger, he traced her collarbone. "And beautiful and wonderful."

Beth decided if she were to die then and there, she'd die happy.

After a few more teasing remarks on his part, which almost led to another session of lovemaking, Beth pushed him away. "Let's go clean up that kitchen first, okay?"

"Slave driver." But he pulled on his jeans and let her get up and put on her robe.

"Oh, dear," Beth said when she saw the forgotten meal she'd prepared sitting on the kitchen table.

"I hate to throw so much food away, but I'd be afraid to eat it. It's been sitting out for hours."

"I'm sorry," Jack said, walking up behind her and putting his arms around her. He lifted her hair and kissed the back of her neck.

Beth wriggled out of his arms. "Now don't start that again, or we'll never get this place cleaned up."

"I was right. You *are* a slave driver."

They made short work of the cleanup, then Beth said, "I can make us some scrambled eggs or grilled cheese sandwiches."

"You farm women don't believe in low cholesterol meals, do you?" Jack teased.

Beth laughed. "I never think about it, to tell the truth."

"In that case, let's have both. I'll make the scrambled eggs, and you can make the grilled cheese."

"He cooks, too?"

"I'm a man of many talents."

"He said modestly."

Jack pretended he was going to swat her behind, but Beth, laughing, twisted away from him.

"Come here, woman," he said with mock severity.

"First I'm a wench and now I'm a woman. Which is it?"

"How about you're a delectable wench and a sexy woman?" Pulling her into his arms, he kissed her. "A *very* sexy woman," he murmured, letting his hands move down to cup her bottom.

"Stop that," she said breathlessly. "Or we'll never eat."

"You said that before."

"Yes, and I was right."

"Okay, okay." Giving her another sound kiss, he patted her behind, then released her.

Companionably, they fixed their meal. Throughout the cooking and the eating and the cleanup, he teased her and she teased back. She reveled in the wordplay. She and Eben had never had fun like this, never teased each other, never talked about sex. This was a new side to Jack, a side she was thoroughly enjoying.

When they finished their second cleanup of the night, they turned out the lights, smiled into each other's eyes and, hand in hand, went back up the stairs.

Chapter Nine

Dee Ann brought the kids home at one o'clock. "We had lunch at Angie's," she said, naming a local pizza place. "So you don't have to worry about feeding them."

"It was so *fun,* Mama," Amy said. "Me and Brittany stayed up till *eleven!*"

"Really?"

Amy nodded her head vigorously. "Uh-*huh.* And we had ice cream and everything. It was so *fun.*"

Beth smothered a smile. "It was so fun," she said to Dee Ann. "Did you have a good time, too, Matthew?"

While the boys were noisily reporting on their sleepover, Dee Ann walked to the refrigerator, opened it, peered inside for a few minutes, then removed a can of soda. Popping the top, she took a long swallow. When the kids finally ran out of steam, she said, "Why don't y'all go play? I want to visit with Beth for a while."

The minute they were gone, she plopped down at the kitchen table. "Well?" She was grinning. "I know you did the deed. I can see it on your face. And I want to hear every delicious detail."

"Dee Ann!" Beth knew her face was flaming.

"Every detail! That's the least you can do when I made the whole thing possible." Her blue eyes were shining with avid curiosity. "Is he a good lover?"

Beth held her hands up as if to ward off a blow. "Oh, no. I'm not going there. That wasn't part of the deal."

"Sure it was. Haven't I shared my love life with you? Such as it is," she added dryly. Then she laughed. "Come on, Beth. Have pity on me. This is the only thrill I'm gonna have, livin' vicariously through you."

Beth rolled her eyes. "Quit exaggerating."

"Don't I wish. You know darn well the last time for me was at least two years ago. At this rate, I'm gonna dry up and wither away. Or forget how to do it. Whichever comes first."

Beth laughed. "Somehow I don't see that happening."

"Yeah, well, I'm gettin' mighty close."

"To withering away? Or forgetting how to do it?"

"Quit trying to change the subject."

"You're always accusing me of that."

"That's because you're always trying to avoid telling me things that as your oldest and dearest friend I have a right to know."

Stalling for time, Beth got a can of soda out of the refrigerator for herself. "I suppose if I don't tell you, you'll sit there forever."

"Yep. Or..." Dee Ann gave Beth a sly smile. "I might just go out and ask Jack."

"You wouldn't!"

"Care to put it to the test?"

Beth knew Dee Ann would never humiliate her by saying anything to Jack, but she also knew her friend would give her no peace until she told her *something*. Sighing, she sat across from Dee Ann. "I'm not giving you details, you can forget that, but yes..." She smiled. "He's a good lover." Her voice softened as images from last night played in her mind. "He's...a wonderful lover."

For a long moment, Dee Ann didn't say anything. Then she, too, sighed. "I'm so jealous. But I'm happy for you, too."

"Thanks. And thanks for making last night possible. You're a good friend."

"Hey, you'd do the same for me, wouldn't you?"

"You know I would."

"Well, then."

They smiled at each other.

"So what do you think?" Dee Ann asked. "Did he say anything, you know, about staying?"

Beth shook her head. She had hoped he might make some kind of commitment to her, but maybe it was too soon. Anyway, the words weren't that important. She knew, just from the way he'd acted, that he cared about her. She also knew he was cautious when it came to his emotions, and she guessed, if she'd been raised the way he was, she'd be cautious, too.

Anyway, even if she was wrong, even if he never did say he loved her, even if he eventually left Rose Hill, she had no real regrets. She'd decided last night that if this was all she ever had with him, it would be enough.

"There's only one other thing I want to know," Dee Ann said. "And then I won't ask another question."

"What?"

She leaned across the table. "How many times did you do it?"

"Dee Ann!"

Dee Ann laughed. "Come on, Beth," she wheedled. "Give me something to fantasize about. It was more than once, wasn't it?"

Beth just shook her head. "You're so bad."

"Twice?"

"I'm not going to answer that. I'm not."

"It was *more* than twice. I know it. I can see it on your face," Dee Ann said triumphantly.

Beth opened her mouth, then closed it. She knew she was blushing again, and she could have kicked herself.

"You can't lie, Beth, so don't even try. Your face is an open book. Now come on, just tell me. I'm not gonna say anything to anyone. Was it three times?"

Actually, it was four times—twice before they came downstairs to eat their midnight supper, once afterward, and then again when they woke up this morning—but even if Dee Ann had held a lighted torch to Beth's bare feet, she wouldn't have admitted it out loud.

"Oh, man! Now I'm *sick* with jealousy! Three times in one night with that gorgeous hunk! And I haven't made love once in two years!" She went on in this vein for a few more minutes, then finally wound down. Draining her drink, she reached for her purse and said, "Well, now that I'm completely demoralized, I'd better get the kids and get going. I have one more appointment today, Mildred Busey, at two-fifteen. And you know how cranky *she* is. If I make her wait, she'll have a fit."

"Did you work this morning?"

"Yeah, two appointments. One at nine, one at ten. Both color touch-ups."

Beth knew Dee Ann tried to keep Saturday appointments at a minimum since the kids were home.

Her shop was set up in her garage, so she was always there for the kids, but even so, she didn't like working when they weren't in school. Summers her mother came and helped her out some, and Billy's mother always took the kids for at least a month, so Dee Ann managed, but it wasn't easy. "Do you want to leave Jason and Brittany here this afternoon?"

"No, that's okay. I promised them after I was through with Mildred, I'd take 'em to a movie. There's a new Disney movie that started yesterday." Dee Ann gave Beth a hug, then went outside to gather up her children.

Beth had nodded when Dee Ann mentioned the Disney movie, but she really didn't pay attention to what movies were playing. It had been so long since she'd had the luxury of taking time off to do anything like that, there seemed to be no point. But if Jack stayed, things would be so differ—

Abruptly she cut off the thought. *Don't count on him. He hasn't said a thing about staying, and if you start believing he's going to, you're just going to end up bitterly disappointed.* But no matter how many times she told herself this, she couldn't stop herself from daydreaming.

It would be so wonderful if Jack *would* stay. If he would ask her to marry him. If they could be a real family, the kind she and the kids had never had—with a father and a mother who loved each other.

Because she *did* love him. She just had not wanted to admit it until now. Beth had always thought, if by some miracle she met someone she could love, that it wouldn't necessarily mean he would be someone she could marry, because not many men were willing to take on another man's children, let alone love them and treat them like their own. And her children's welfare and happiness had to come before Beth's. Actually, Beth could never *be* happy if her children weren't.

But that wasn't a concern with Jack. He was wonderful with the kids. He had more patience than she did. Unlike many adults, he actually listened to what they had to say, and he answered their questions endlessly. It was obvious that he really liked them, maybe even more than liked them. The way he treated them was a big part of the reason Beth found him so appealing. She didn't think she'd ever have to worry that he would resent them or mistreat them.

She sighed. It would be so great—the four of them together. She could just picture them this winter. After supper, Jack would light a fire in the fireplace and in the evenings they would sit there together. His arm would be around her and the kids would be playing checkers on the floor. Maybe they'd be eating popcorn or drinking hot chocolate. Every once in a while, Jack would nuzzle her neck and whisper in her ear, and then they'd smile at each other because they'd know that soon it would be time to go to bed.

She thought about Christmas. How lonely last Christmas had been, and how wonderful it would be to have Jack there this year. How they'd all go out to the Christmas tree farm and cut down their own tree, then bring it home and Jack would get it in the stand while Beth got out the boxes of ornaments. They'd let the kids help them decorate the tree, and Beth would tell Jack the history of each ornament—some of which had been handed down by her great-grandmother—and that night they'd sit in the dark with the tree lights on and maybe some Christmas carols playing softly in the background.

She was in the midst of this rosy fantasy when Matthew came running up the back steps and into the kitchen.

"Mom," Matthew said. "Jack wants to know if you need anything in town."

"Oh? Is he going in?"

"Uh-huh."

"Well, let me think. Tell him I'll make a list."

"Okay."

After Matthew went racing back to the barn, Beth started checking her supplies. She was out of paper towels and was low on milk. She could also use some apples. As she wrote these items down and continued to look in her cupboards, she wondered why Jack was going to town at all. She didn't think they needed anything for the farm.

List in hand, she walked out to the barn. She could see he'd been working on building a trellis.

He looked up when she entered. Pure happiness flooded her as their eyes met, and he smiled. She wished they were alone, but Matthew was standing right next to Jack, watching everything he did, and Amy was sitting on an overturned crate nearby. She wondered if Jack would have kissed her if the kids hadn't been there.

"Here's my list," she said, handing him the paper.

He scanned it, then nodded. "Okay. Anything else?"

"Not that I can think of." She wanted to ask him what he was going to do in town, though she knew she didn't have any right to. But it *was* kind of funny that he hadn't offered the information. *What happened between the two of you last night doesn't mean you own him, Beth.* Well, she knew that. Still, he usually *did* tell her what errands he planned to run.

"I should be back by three," he said.

"All right."

"Can I go with you, Jack?" Matthew said.

Because Beth was watching Jack's face, she saw the flash of consternation, which he quickly masked. Before he could say anything, she said, "Matthew, you just got home. Besides, you and your sister have some chores to do."

Matthew started to protest, but Beth gave him

one of her looks—the one that said *don't argue with me*.

"Oh, okay," he said glumly.

Jack ruffled Matthew's hair. "Another time, okay?"

Matthew nodded and the glum look disappeared.

"I was thinking, how about if I pick up something for supper? Give you a break from cooking," Jack said. His eyes met hers.

Beth's heart gave a little happy skip. He'd been thinking about her, just as she'd been thinking about him. "That would be nice."

"Do you like Chinese food?"

"I do, but the kids don't."

"I like Chinese food," Matthew said.

"Since when?" But Beth knew. If Jack had suggested sushi or Polynesian food or liver, Matthew would have said he liked it, even though he'd never eaten any of them.

"I could get something like Lemon Chicken and plenty of rice. They'd probably like that," Jack suggested. "And I'll bet they'd like fried dumplings."

"Fried dumplings?" Amy said. "Mama makes dumplings, but she doesn't *fry* 'em."

"You make dumplings?" Jack said. "You're a woman of many talents."

Their eyes met again, and Beth knew he was thinking about last night. She was glad for the filtered light in the barn, because once again, she knew she was blushing.

"My mom's dumplings are the *best!*" Matthew declared proudly.

"Maybe one of these days she'll make them for me."

Beth wet her lips. "I usually make them on the first really cold day of winter." *Will you be here then?*

"I'm looking forward to it," Jack said softly.

Leaving Jack to put away his tools and get ready to go to town, Beth and the children headed for the house. Beth's heart was singing. Everything Jack had said, every look he'd given her, told her that what had happened between them last night meant as much to him as it had to her.

Maybe he was going to stay after all.

Jack knew from the moment he awakened that morning that he was going to have to tell Beth the truth as quickly as possible. But before he did, he wanted to talk to Cord. He'd had an idea and wanted to be sure Cord was willing to go along with it.

On the drive in to Tyler, he thought about last night. It had been incredible. *Beth* was incredible. He'd guessed she was a passionate woman. And she was, but that was only part of the story. She was also incredibly giving. Giving and open and honest. She held nothing back. And, in turn, Jack wanted to be the same way with her. Yet he'd known he couldn't be until there were no secrets or falsehoods between them.

So though he was nervous about confessing how he'd deceived her, even scared, he knew it was something that must be done, and right away.

In Tyler, he stopped at the first pay phone he found. Two minutes later, Cord was on the line.

"Am I glad you called!" Cord said.

"Why? Do you have news?"

"Yes. Kate and Brett finally were able to talk with Madelyn LeClaire, and she admitted she was our mother and she wants to see us."

Even though Jack thought he'd been prepared for this, his heart knocked against his rib cage at Cord's announcement. "Are Kate and Brett still in France?"

Weeks ago, when Kate and Brett first arrived in Massachusetts, they'd discovered that Madelyn LeClaire and her husband and daughter had gone to the south of France. Upon investigation, they found out the family had a villa there and that was where they spent their winters. Jack had known all this because he called Cord every Saturday to get an update on their progress. Until now, there had been nothing to report.

"No," Cord said, "they're on their way to Cape Cod. So are Rafe and Caroline. Hannah and I waited for your phone call, but we're planning to leave in the morning. We were hoping you'd come with us."

"What about our...mother?"

"Madelyn, Brandon and Hope—who, by the way, is really our sister and not our half sister—are already back in Chatham."

"Did Kate get any kind of explanation out of them? Like why the hell we never heard from them?" He knew the bitterness he always tried to pretend didn't exist was now evident from his tone.

Cord's normally brusque, businesslike speaking voice, softened. "Kate said we needed to hear everything firsthand. That it would be impossible for her to relay everything that had been said between her and our mother, and anyway, she didn't think it was her place to tell Madelyn's story."

Jack guessed that made sense. But he wasn't going to be a pushover just because Madelyn LeClaire really was his mother. She didn't need to think she could feed them some cock-and-bull story and that he'd just swallow it and forget that she had abandoned them. Besides, it took more than giving birth to a child to call yourself his mother. That title needed to be *earned*. So if she thought he was going to fall into her arms, she had another think coming.

"So?" Cord said into the silence. "Are you going with us?"

"Yes, I'm going. I'll be in Grandview by five. Are you going to make a reservation for me?"

"It's already made."

"You were confident."

"No, Jack, I never take you for granted. I just believe in preparing for every contingency."

Jack grunted. He was spoiling for a fight, anything to give vent to the anger that was building inside him, but Cord wasn't the one upon whom to spill it. *Save it,* he told himself. *Save it for the person who really deserves it.* "All right, thanks," he finally said. "I'll see you later today."

After the conversation with Cord, Jack did the grocery shopping, then found a Chinese restaurant. Even though he wasn't going to be there now, he had promised to bring food back for supper.

What was he going to tell Beth? He wished he could tell her the truth, but that would require a lot of time and explanation, because he sure didn't want to just dump it on her, then leave. Hell, it could take hours. Maybe even days. Who knew *how* she'd take the news that not only had he been lying to her all these weeks, but that he was a member of the despised Stockwell family.

He couldn't tell her the truth. Not today. He guessed the best thing to do was give her as little information as possible and explain everything when he came back. It wasn't an ideal solution, but it was the best he could come up with at the moment.

While Jack was gone, Beth cleaned house. It wasn't a chore she loved, but today she didn't mind it at all. Not even when she got to the bathroom, which was her least favorite job of all. Of course, today she didn't mind much, she thought happily, humming as she worked.

The kids were helping, too. They were picking up their own rooms, and Matthew was also going to dust the living room and dining room. Once again, she thought what good kids she had.

Beth was in the middle of scrubbing the tub when she heard Jack's truck coming down the driveway. Peering out, she saw him pull around to the back and begin unloading grocery bags. Hurriedly she dried her hands, then raced downstairs.

She pushed the screen door open. "I heard you coming," she said, smiling down at him.

His return smile seemed strained, and when he didn't quite meet her eyes, she knew something was wrong. Walking inside, he set the two bags of groceries on the kitchen table. "I've got the Chinese food out in the truck. I'll bring it in."

Beth started putting away the groceries while he went outside to get the food for their supper. She tried to tell herself she was imagining a problem where none existed. But she couldn't shake her growing feeling of dread.

A few minutes later, Jack returned with the plastic bag of food. He placed it on the counter and looked at her.

"Smells good." She hadn't been imagining anything. His eyes told her he was troubled. Because she was afraid, she began to fiddle with the bag, which had been tied at the top.

"Beth."

She stopped fooling with the bag and looked up. God, his eyes were blue.

"Something's come up, and I'm not going to be here for supper."

"Oh."

"The thing is, I have to go away for a few days."

"Go away?" she repeated faintly.

"I'm sorry. I know it's short notice, but there's something important I have to take care of."

On the outside, Beth tried to act as if his announcement hadn't just shaken her to her core. Inside, she was trembling. What was he really trying to tell her? Was he going away for good? Had she been wrong about *everything?* Remembering last night, remembering the things they'd done, the things *she'd* done, she wanted to die.

When she didn't say anything, he continued, a pleading note in his voice. "I wish I could explain, but I can't. I won't be gone long. A couple of days at the most. And when I get back, I'll tell you everything. I promise."

Other people had made promises to Beth, too. And those promises had been broken.

"Ah, Beth," he said, reaching out to touch her cheek. "Don't look like that. I know this looks bad, coming right now, but it can't be helped."

She wanted to believe him. She wanted more

than anything to believe him. But she was so afraid. If he would just tell her *why* he was leaving and where he was going, maybe then she might be able to, but he hadn't, had he?

He looked as if he wanted to add something else, but he didn't. He just bent down, kissed her cheek, said, "I've gotta go put away some things in the barn, then get my stuff packed. I'll come back and say goodbye to the kids when I'm ready to go." And then he walked out the door.

Beth fought against the tears that welled up in her eyes. She remembered what she'd thought earlier. *Even if Jack leaves Rose Hill, if last night is all I ever have, it'll be enough.* Had she really *believed* that?

No, of course she hadn't.

She had believed he was going to stay. She had believed he loved her. That it would just take some time, but he would eventually realize it and tell her. She had never thought he would actually leave.

But she was wrong.

And now he was going.

For all she knew, this might be the last time she would ever see him. A sob tore through her, and she wanted to run outside and grab hold of him. Beg him not to go. She clenched her fists. *Please, God,* she prayed, *please don't let this happen.*

"Mama?"

Beth swallowed and hurriedly swiped the tears from her eyes before turning around. Amy stood in the doorway, her Pooh bear in her arms. Her little face wore an expression of concern. "Oh, hi, sweetie. I thought you were upstairs." Even to Beth's ears, her voice sounded strange.

Amy stared at her. "Are you sad, Mama?"

Beth should have known she couldn't fool her daughter. "Oh, maybe. Just a little."

"I'm sorry." Amy walked over and put her arms around Beth. Her head only came to Beth's waist.

Her daughter's sympathy was almost Beth's undoing. Yet somehow she managed to keep from falling apart. That would come later, she knew. When she was alone.

Right now, though, she had to do the acting job of her life, not only for Amy's and Matthew's sake—for both children were going to be crushed by Jack's departure—but for the sake of her own pride.

Forcing a casual brightness into her voice, she ruffled Amy's hair. "Sweetie, go call Matthew and tell him to come downstairs, okay? Jack's going away for a while, but he said he wanted to say goodbye to the two of you."

Amy frowned. "Jack's going away?"

"Yes. He has to leave."

"But he's coming back, isn't he?"

I hope so. "Yes, he's coming back. He just has to go and take care of some business." She made herself laugh. "That's what adults do. They take care of business."

"Oh. Okay." But Amy's forehead was still wrinkled with worry.

"Now go call Matthew, okay?"

A few minutes later Matthew burst into the kitchen. "Is Amy telling the truth, Mom? Is Jack really leaving?"

"Just for a while, honey." She knew her smile wasn't her best, but it was all she could manage. "Why don't you and Amy go on out and say goodbye to him. I think he's in the barn."

She watched as the two children ran outside. Once they disappeared into the barn, she left the kitchen and slowly headed back upstairs and into the bathroom. Kneeling in front of the tub, she picked up her scrub brush and continued with her interrupted task. But as hard as she scrubbed, she couldn't scrub away the knowledge that in just a few minutes, Jack would walk out of her life. Maybe for good.

Chapter Ten

Jack reached the mansion in record time. During the drive, he tried not to think about Beth, but he couldn't help it. He hated remembering the hurt look in her eyes and the knowledge that he'd put it there.

It couldn't be helped, though. At this point, the best he could hope for was that when he got back to Rose Hill and explained everything to her, she would understand and forgive him.

As always, when he saw the Stockwell mansion again after not having seen it for a while, he was struck by its pretentiousness, the way it screamed that the owner had far more money than taste. It was such an extravagant waste. Who in the hell needed forty rooms, anyway? When Jack thought of the way millions of people all over the world were lucky to even have indoor plumbing, when he thought about all the starving children he'd seen in so many war-torn countries, when he remembered the distended bellies, the sickness and the look of despair in their eyes, then came face-to-face with this Greek Revival monstrosity and gaudy display of wealth, it disgusted him.

He knew, though, that he was the only one of his siblings who felt this way. Of course, to be fair, the others had not seen what he'd seen over the past dozen years, either. But even if they had—as Cord had pointed out when Jack had recently criticized the family's excesses—one family could hardly solve all the world's ills. And Jack was realist enough to know Cord was right.

Hell, we can't even solve our own problems, he thought. He drove his truck around to the bank of garages which mostly housed Cord's collection of sports cars. Relinquishing the truck to Ned Fisher, the family's longtime driver-mechanic, Jack grabbed his duffel bag and strode toward the back of the house.

One of the kitchen maids, flustered when she saw who had rung the bell, let him in.

"Why, Mr. Jack, we were looking for you out the front."

"Hello, Daisy." Jack was glad he'd remembered the girl's name. "Is Cord in?"

"Oh, yes, sir. He's expectin' you. He's in his office."

After greeting the cook and another of the maids, Jack headed for the west wing, which housed the offices of Stockwell, International. He found Cord's office door open and Cord seated behind his desk. He was talking to someone on the speaker phone. Cord grinned and waved at Jack, motioning for him to take a seat.

"I'll be off in a minute," he mouthed.

Jack nodded. Dropping the duffel onto the floor, he sat in one of the four leather chairs grouped around Cord's desk.

"So whatta you think, Cord?" a male voice boomed from the speaker. "You gonna do this deal with us?"

"Sure, Walt. Count me in," Cord said.

"That's great. You won't be sorry. We're gonna make us a big pile of money."

"Good. Let me know when the paperwork is ready."

They said their goodbyes and Cord disconnected the call. Standing up, he came around to Jack. Jack stood and extended his hand, but Cord surprised him by putting his arms around him and hugging him. For a moment, Jack didn't respond—they'd never been a demonstrative family—then slowly, he returned his brother's embrace.

"Good to see you," Cord said.

"You, too."

Instead of going back to his chair behind the desk, Cord sat opposite Jack in one of the leather chairs. Propping one loafer-shod foot on the rung of a neighboring chair, he sat back and studied Jack. For a moment, neither spoke. Then, surprising Jack again, Cord said, "You angry about all this, Jack?"

"What makes you say that?" Jack countered.

"I don't know. You sounded a little upset when we talked earlier."

For a moment, Jack didn't say anything. When he finally responded, his voice was tight. "Yeah, you could say I'm a little angry. I mean, hell, it isn't every day a man finds out his mother is alive and well, yet cared so damn little about him or her other kids she completely ignored them for twenty-nine years."

"C'mon, Jack, we don't know the whole story yet. Don't you think you should give her the benefit of the doubt until we do?"

Jack shrugged. "I'll listen to what she has to say, sure."

"But will it be with an open mind?"

Jack's lips tightened. He couldn't imagine what Madelyn LeClaire could say that would vindicate her actions.

"She *is* our mother," Cord said softly.

"Since when have you turned into such a bleeding heart?"

Cord smiled. "I'd hardly classify myself as a bleeding heart."

"All right. Let me rephrase that. Since when have you become so soft?"

"If that was meant to insult me, it isn't going to work. Anyway, I don't think I'm soft. I just have a better understanding of some things than I had before I became a husband and father." Cord's voice turned tender. "You know, Jack, there's nothing quite like the patter of little feet and the love of a good woman to change a man."

Jack wanted to make fun of the goofy look on Cord's face. But then he remembered Beth. Beth and Matthew and Amy. How could he make fun of Cord, when he wanted what Cord had? He knew the only reason he would make fun of his brother was because he was envious.

"Did I hear someone talking about me?"

Both men looked around. Cord's wife, Hannah, with little Becky in her arms, stood in the doorway. She was smiling and Becky, the moment she spied her father, tried to wriggle out of her mother's hold.

Cord got up, walked over to his wife, gave her a lingering kiss on the mouth, then lifted the baby out of her arms. Becky patted his face happily, and Cord chuckled. "She loves her daddy. Don't you, sugar?" He kissed the baby soundly, too, then pointed to Jack. "Want to give Uncle Jack a kiss?"

Although Jack had never considered himself a baby man, he couldn't deny seven-month-old Becky's attractions. She was chubby and dimpled and beautiful, with dark blue Stockwell eyes and dark, curly hair. She held her fat little arms out to Jack, inviting his kiss. Something tugged at his heart when he inhaled the sweet baby smell and felt her soft cheek against his. A sudden image of another baby—one that would have his eyes and Beth's hair—assaulted him, and for the second time in five minutes, he felt a painful stab of envy. Cord had everything: a beautiful wife who loved him and a beautiful daughter. Everything Jack had finally realized he wanted but was afraid he'd never have.

Later that night, after Becky had been put to bed, the three adults had a quiet dinner and discussed the next day's plans.

"Our flight leaves DFW at nine in the morning," Cord said. "Ned'll drive us to the airport."

"Why aren't we using the company jet?"

"It's in for servicing. Phil's waiting on a part."

Jack nodded. "We flying into Boston?"

"Yes. From there we'll take a small charter out to the Cape. I booked a limo to get us from the airport to Chatham."

"You think of everything."

Cord grinned. "I try."

"When's the meeting with…our mother…set up?" Jack still had a hard time saying the words *our mother*.

"I think we're supposed to go out there tomorrow night."

For the rest of their meal, they talked about inconsequential things, and Jack was glad. He didn't want to talk about tomorrow.

After dinner, Cord and Hannah said their goodnights.

"I'm sorry to be leavin' you on your own tonight," Hannah apologized in her soft Oklahoma drawl, "but Becky gets up awful early, so we turn in early, too."

Cord's eyes met Jack's. In them Jack saw amusement, but he also saw something else, something that said Cord was contented and happy. That he didn't mind giving up his wild, single days. That going to bed early was a pleasure, not a duty. That he and his lovely wife looked forward to their time together in that opulent bedroom upstairs. Of course, Jack didn't know that the bedroom was still opulent. Probably wasn't, as a matter of fact. He was sure down-to-earth Hannah had made plenty of changes in the decor, just as she had in her husband.

"That's okay," Jack said. "I'll probably come on up in a little while myself."

Jack headed for the library after his brother and his wife had gone upstairs to their suite. He fixed himself a stiff bourbon and water and turned out all the lights but one. Someone had made a fire in the fireplace to ward off the chill of the first blue norther to hit the Dallas area this year, and Jack sank into a big leather armchair, propped his feet on an ottoman and stared into the flames as he nursed his drink.

He didn't know how he felt about going to Massachusetts tomorrow. Part of him was glad there would finally be some closure for his family. But the other part of him, the part that had been hurt so many times over the years, wasn't sure he ever wanted to see the woman who had deserted them.

And yet…somewhere deep inside was a yearning that he couldn't deny. He hated this weakness in himself, had tried to overcome it, but still it remained.

Sighing deeply, he finished his drink, then headed up to his own suite of rooms.

For a moment after waking on Sunday morning, Beth was happy. Then she remembered that Jack was gone, and her heart plummeted.

What if he never came back?

She bit her lip. Closed her eyes. Oh, God. How would she bear it?

The same way you've borne everything else that's happened to you in your life, Elizabeth Lillian. You'll put your chin up, and you'll get on with it.

The words were vivid enough in her mind that it was almost as if her grandmother was there and had spoken them aloud.

"But I love him so much, Granny," she whispered, "so very much."

Yes, darlin', I know you do. And I loved your grandfather with all my heart, and when he died I

*thought I'd die to. But I didn't. We Wilder women
are made of stern stuff, and you're a Wilder.*

Yes, Beth thought, that's what her grandmother
would say if she were here. And her grandmother
was right. Beth would survive if Jack never returned, because she had to. She had two young children to think about, and they needed her. Telling
herself to get up and stop feeling sorry for herself,
she climbed out of bed and prepared to face the
day.

"I love flying first-class," Hannah said midway
through their flight. She and Becky were sitting
across the aisle from Cord and Jack.

Although Jack would never have admitted it to
anyone, so did he. This was an aspect of his personality he wasn't proud of; it didn't fit with his
image of himself. But secretly, he enjoyed every
minute of the pampering you got when you held a
first-class ticket.

They arrived at Boston's Logan Airport a little
after three. The charter was ready and waiting for
them. The flight to the Cape was a short one, so
just after four, they were comfortably ensconced in
the limousine Cord had booked and on their way to
the hotel in Chatham.

Jack emptied his mind and stared out at the scen-
ery whizzing by. At times they were in full view
of the water, at others the road dipped farther inland
or a small rise would hide the shore. It was his first

visit to Cape Cod, and from what he could see, descriptions of the place hadn't been exaggerated. It was beautiful. He tried to imagine growing up there, but that conjured up memories he'd rather forget, so he tried not to think along those lines.

By four-thirty the limo was parked under the porte cochere of the seaside inn where the family was staying.

As Cord and Jack were checking in, Jack heard his sister calling his name.

"I was just coming down to watch for you," she said, throwing her arms around him and giving him a hug. Her blue eyes sparkled, and Jack thought she looked happier than he'd seen her look in a long time. He was relieved. He'd been afraid Kate harbored some of the same anger he'd been feeling for the past twenty-four hours.

After hugging Cord and Hannah, Kate commandeered Becky, and in between cooing at her and giving her kisses, she filled them in on plans for the evening's meeting.

"Uncle Brandon has asked that you come early to meet with him first, Jack."

"Oh? Why?"

Kate shrugged. "I don't know. He just said he had to talk with you first. He asked that you go out to the house at six. We're to follow at seven."

"Have you seen her yet?" They both knew who he meant by *her*.

Kate shook her head, and some of the happiness in her eyes faded. "I think she's scared to see us."

"I don't blame her," Cord said.

Jack was getting irritated with Cord's attitude. Wasn't he the least *bit* angry? Hell, the way he was acting, you'd think it was an everyday, normal occurrence for a mother to walk out on her children!

Finished with check-in, the entourage followed the bellman into the elevator.

"Where's your room?" Hannah asked Kate.

"We're all on the third floor." She nuzzled Becky's neck, which made the baby giggle. "Oh, she's so *darling,* Hannah. I want one just like her."

Hannah smiled proudly.

Sometimes it was hard for Jack to remember that Hannah wasn't Becky's birth mother, she so obviously doted on the child.

Arriving on three, everyone trooped off the elevator and down the hall.

"This is Brett's and my room," Kate said, stopping in front of Room 310. "Rafe and Caroline are across the hall in 311."

The bellman stopped in front of Room 312. "This is our room," Cord said to Hannah.

Jack looked at his key. He was in Room 313.

The next few minutes were taken up with unloading luggage, tipping the bellman, greeting Brett, Rafe and Caroline, and getting oriented.

"Does *anyone* know why our uncle wants to see me first?" Jack asked.

Rafe shook his head and Brett shrugged.

"You *are* the oldest," Kate pointed out. "Maybe that's why. But that doesn't make sense, does it?"

"No." But nothing about this whole affair made sense to Jack. "So is someone going to take me there?"

"I will," Rafe said.

"All right. What time?"

"They don't live far from here. Ten minutes at the most. How about if we leave about a quarter of six?"

Jack looked at his watch. It was already close to five. "In that case, I'm going to leave you all and go shower and change."

"All right. Just come next door when you're ready."

At exactly 5:45 p.m., Jack knocked on Rafe and Caroline's door. Rafe must have been standing on the other side, for it immediately opened. Blowing a kiss to his wife, he said, "I'll be back in about thirty minutes."

"Bye, sweetie," she said.

Jack wasn't sure how much of this newly hitched euphoria he could stand. Cord and Hannah, Kate and Brett, Rafe and Caroline. He wondered what Beth would think of them—these siblings of his. He knew what they'd think of her. They would love her. Who wouldn't? But would they ever have the opportunity to meet her? He hated when his thoughts turned dark and gloomy, but he couldn't seem to keep them steered in a positive direction.

Jack barely noticed the picturesque town as Rafe drove down the main street, then turned in the direction of the Sound. One turn, another, and then they were there, and he was pulling the rented Mercedes in front of a well-cared-for white clapboard two-story house with black shutters. The gated front yard was filled with roses, the irony of which was not lost on Jack. For a moment, Jack didn't move. "You okay?" Rafe said, turning to look at him.

Jack nodded. But he wasn't okay. Just looking at this house, at this beautiful setting, had caused a surge of anger so intense he was shaking inside.

"See you later, then."

Fighting to master his emotions, Jack got out of the car and Rafe drove off. Jack studied his surroundings. Behind the house, perhaps a hundred yards away, lay Nantucket Sound. The water glowed a deep reddish orange from the setting sun. The air smelled like the ocean, fresh and salty, and was filled with the sound of the surf and squawking gulls. He couldn't see the beach because the house sat on a small rise.

Opening the gate, Jack walked up the brick path that led to the front door. A sudden cool gust of wind whipped his pant legs. He rang the bell.

A few moments later the front door opened. Because he'd been expecting his uncle, Jack was surprised to be staring into the blue eyes of the young woman from the painting—the young woman he now knew was his sister. She was dressed in a dark blue dress that skimmed her slender frame. Even if Jack hadn't been told Hope LeClaire was related to him, he'd have known it just by looking at her, for she looked so much like Kate, there could be no doubt they were sisters. She smiled Kate's smile and held out her hands. "You're Jack."

"Yes."

"I'm Hope."

Later, Jack would never remember what he'd said in response. Although his head had known he was going to be meeting his youngest sister, his heart hadn't been prepared for the emotions that swept through him like an avalanche. She must have realized he was overcome, because she squeezed his hands and said, "Come in. Please."

She drew him into a small entryway. To the left was a formal living room and to the right was a formal dining room, as well as stairs that led to the second story. Straight ahead, a closed door kept him from seeing the back of the house.

Jack finally found his voice. "I'm sorry. I guess I just feel a bit stunned."

"It's okay. I understand. I feel the same way."

Jack saw that her blue eyes shone with tears. At the sight, his shock subsided, to be replaced by the same tenderness Jack felt when he was with Kate. This was his sister! "Please don't cry," he said softly. "I'm no good around tears."

She smiled and brushed the tears away. "We'll talk later, okay? Right now my dad's anxious to see you. He's in the living room, waiting."

Jack nodded and started to turn toward the open doorway.

"Wait," she said. "Before you go in, there's something you should know. He's almost completely blind."

"Oh. I'm...I'm sorry."

"Yes," Hope said sadly, "we all are."

"What happened?"

"An accident before I was born."

"Can he see anything at all?"

"Mostly just shapes and shadows. Nothing specific."

Jack nodded. "Thanks for telling me."

Hope touched his arm. Her eyes met his. "I'm so glad you're here."

Jack smiled down at her, then, impulsively, he put his arms around her and hugged her. "I am, too." And at that moment, he meant it.

Jack stared down at the man sitting in the wheelchair in front of the bay window. He had known Brandon was his father's twin, but he hadn't been prepared to see the uncanny likeness in the flesh. Once more, his emotions were tumultuous. "Uncle Brandon?" he said.

His uncle smiled. "Jack!" Both the smile and his voice were filled with a welcoming warmth, a warmth Jack had never seen in Caine. "I'm glad you're here," he added, echoing Hope's words almost exactly. "Please. Have a seat."

Jack sat across from his uncle in a chintz-covered armchair. The room was very attractive, filled with antiques and brightly cushioned furniture. Flowers were everywhere, and a bright fire burned in the small fireplace on the opposite wall.

"Would you like a drink?" Brandon asked. "There's brandy and Scotch and bourbon on that pine chest in the corner." He gestured toward the far end of the room. "And some glasses in that cabinet next to it. I'd get it for you, but—"

"That's all right," Jack said. "I don't mind. Do you want anything?" Belatedly he saw the crystal tumbler on a table nearby.

"I have a drink, thanks."

Jack walked over to the cabinet, took out a matching tumbler, then poured himself a small quantity of brandy. He took his time, and by the time he was seated again, he felt calmer and more in control. He wished he could see Brandon's eyes, but they were hidden by tinted glasses. Did the glasses help with glare? Jack wondered. Or did they hide the evidence of his blindness?

"I wish I could see you properly," his uncle said.

"I'm not much to see."

"I'm sure that's not true. Your mother told me you were the most handsome boy she'd ever seen."

At the mention of Madelyn, Jack could feel his insides tensing. Where was she? he wondered. "I don't remember her," he said stiffly. But that wasn't true. He *did* remember her. The clouds of dark hair. The way she smelled, sweet, like flowers. The way she felt when she hugged him and kissed him good-night. He swallowed.

"I'm sorry," Brandon said softly.

Sorry doesn't cut it, Jack thought. The sympathy he'd started to feel for his uncle disappeared. *Don't be taken in because he's old and nearly blind. Remember. He ran off with your mother. They left you and your brothers and sister, and they never looked back!*

"Jack, I know how you must feel."

"No, you don't," Jack said, allowing his voice to show the anger inside him.

Brandon sighed. "I don't blame you for feeling the way you do. In your shoes, I would be angry, too. That's one of the reasons I wanted to talk to you first. The other is because there's something you need to know. Something that doesn't affect your brothers and sister."

"Oh?"

"You have a right to be angry. The only thing I'm asking of you right now is that you give me a chance to tell you what happened all those years ago."

"I know what happened."

"You only think you do. Will you listen?"

"I'm here."

"Okay then. You know that Caine and I are—*were*—identical twins. We were always very competitive. Not so much in a business sense, or anything, but in other ways, Caine perhaps more so than I. He always had to be the best at everything. If I mastered a jump with Rocky—Rocky was our horse—he had to master a more difficult one. If I beat him playing tennis, he would insist upon playing until he'd beaten me twice, or three times. Same way with girls. If I had a crush on a girl and he found out, he'd ask her out. He simply couldn't stand me getting the better of him in any way."

"That doesn't surprise me," Jack said.

"You know, I'm sure, that your mother was the daughter of our housekeeper, Emily Johnson."

Jack wasn't sure he *had* known that.

"When Emily died, Madelyn took over her duties. She was very young, but she did a wonderful job. Everyone in the household loved her. Including me," he added softly. "I was thrilled when she said she felt the same way about me."

"This was *before* my mother married my father?"

"Yes, this was before she married Caine."

"Did my father know about this?"

Brandon smiled wryly. "Oh, yes, he knew." The smile faded, and his voice became serious again. "One night I talked to Caine about my feelings. I told him I was in love with your mother and wanted to marry her. I told him I'd been thinking about the land our grandfather had supposedly stolen from her family and that I thought we should try to make restitution.''

Jack took a swallow of brandy.

''Caine adamantly refused. I tried everything I could think of to persuade him to change his mind, and finally he said he'd think about it.''

Jack grunted in disbelief.

''Yes, you're right. He had no intention of changing his mind. He just wanted to get me off his back. Anyway, unbeknownst to me, a couple of days later he found your mother crying. He asked her what was wrong, and she, not knowing any better, confessed that she was pregnant with my child. She said she was afraid to tell me because she wasn't sure I wanted to marry her, and she didn't want to force me. You see, I hadn't said anything about us getting married, because I wanted to try to make things right first. That was my first mistake.''

Jack sat frozen as the import of Brandon's words slowly sank in. Was it possible? No. What he was thinking couldn't be possible. It couldn't be.

''My second mistake was trusting my brother. You see, what he did was tell Madelyn he would talk to me. That I was honorable and he was sure I would marry her when I knew about the baby. That she should go to her room and wait to hear from him. Later he sent her a note asking her if she would be ready to elope the next night, if necessary. Madelyn sent back a note back saying yes. In the meantime, he told me that he was very sorry, but Madelyn had been leading me on. He said it was really him she loved and that one night while I was away, she had slept with him, and now she was pregnant with his child. He said she had just agreed to marry him, that they were going away to be married the following day. Then he showed me the two notes.''

Suddenly Jack could stand it no longer. He jumped up. ''What are you saying?'' he demanded in a hoarse voice.

Brandon looked up. ''Something I've wanted to tell you for a long time. Caine wasn't your father. I'm your father.''

Chapter Eleven

Sunday night, after the kids were in bed, Beth called Dee Ann.

"Who died?" Dee Ann asked when she heard Beth's woebegone voice.

"Nobody died."

"Well, you sure sound like somebody did. What's wrong?"

So Beth told her, ending with, "I just have this awful feeling that he's not ever coming back."

"Beth, you're jumping to conclusions. He *said* he'd be back, didn't he?"

"Yes, but why wouldn't he tell me where he was going?"

"Oh, shoot, who knows? It has to do with control. Men like to feel they're calling the shots, and if they have to tell you everything, they're somehow losing their manhood.''

In spite of herself, Beth laughed.

''That's better,'' Dee Ann said. ''Seriously, give him a chance. I mean, if he's still not back in a week, *then* I'd start worrying, but right now he's only been gone a day. It's *way* too soon to be concerned.''

''You're probably right.''

''Hell, girl, I know I'm right.''

Beth was glad she'd called. Dee Ann always made her feel better.

''Tell you what,'' Dee Ann said. ''Why don't you and the kids have supper with us tomorrow night?''

''Oh, I don't know. I hate to leave the farm unattended. What if something happens with the misting system?''

''Honestly, Beth, you are such a mother hen! Nothing's going to happen to your roses because you're gone a couple of hours. Now come on. No sense sitting there brooding.''

''Oh, all right.''

''Good. Be here at six. I'll make my world-famous Parmesan Chicken.''

Jack was shaking. He stared down at the stranger seated before him and tried to digest what he'd just heard. His father? Brandon was his father?

"I know you're shocked."

Even *shocked* seemed too mild a word to describe what Jack was feeling. "H-how long have you known this?" he finally managed to get out.

"Please, Jack, sit down. Let me finish, okay? Then, if you want to yell at me or hit me or even if you just want to walk out of here and never come back, I won't blame you."

Jack sank back into his chair. He couldn't seem to take it in. He'd heard the words, but they hadn't really penetrated. Not completely. He picked up his brandy glass and drained it. The liquid burned as it went down, but Jack hardly noticed.

Quietly Brandon resumed his story. "When Caine told me he and Madelyn were getting married, that she loved *him* and not me, that she'd just used me to make him jealous, I was devastated. I wouldn't have believed him except for that note and her answer. To me, that was proof. Damning proof."

Jack was having a hard time focusing on Brandon's story, yet he knew he had to hear everything before he would know how he really felt.

"Caine said the best thing for all of us would be for me to leave. He told me a job had opened up in the Middle East—overseeing one of our former oil operations that was now in the control of the Arab government. They needed a consultant and were offering a great deal of money to anyone who would come and work with them. It was a five-year commitment. I jumped at it. I knew I couldn't stay in Grandview. How could I be around Madelyn every day knowing she was going to marry Caine? So I packed my bags and left immediately without saying goodbye to anyone.''

"And…'' Jack wet his dry lips. "And my mother just married Caine? Without any questions?''

"You have to understand. She was very young and very vulnerable. Caine convinced her I'd betrayed her. He said when he told me about the baby, I told him I didn't believe her baby was mine. Then he told her that even though I didn't love her, he did and he wanted to marry her. He promised her a life of happiness and security, for both her and her child. He said no one would ever know you weren't his son, that he would recognize you as his firstborn, and you would have all the privileges that went along with that recognition.

"She was distraught, completely crushed by my abandonment. She had no money of her own, no skills other than housekeeping. What else could she do? She thought marriage to Caine was the only solution.''

Yes, Jack could understand how this could happen. He'd seen Caine manipulate others in just the same way.

"Caine sent me a telegram the day after their marriage. You know, Jack, the funny thing is, I never blamed him. Not then. I blamed myself for believing in a woman who didn't deserve my trust.''

"How did you find out the truth?" Jack said. He felt calmer now. Almost detached.

Brandon took a sip of his brandy. "It took a while. I stayed in the Middle East for those five years, only hearing from Caine sporadically. When that assignment was over and the Arabs I was working with wanted me to stay on another year, I did. I was making a lot of money and I figured, why not? Even after that next year was over, I didn't go home. I traveled around Europe, had some fun. By now I'd been gone nearly seven years. You were six years old, and in the meantime, your mother and Caine had had three more children. I was finally over her, I thought, and felt I could handle going home, handle seeing her again.''

His voice had grown hoarse, and he cleared his throat. "When I arrived back in Grandview, I was unprepared for how I would feel when I saw your mother again." His voice grew softer. "She was so incredibly beautiful. Different from the way I remembered her, poised and more confident. She was also a very talented artist. Later I found out she'd begun studying art soon after I left as an outlet for her loneliness. Despite all these outer changes, she was still the same sweet, generous, kind woman she'd always been. Anyone could see that. I didn't want to see it. I wanted to believe she was hard, a gold digger who had believed Caine was the better prize. But I couldn't. All you had to do was see how she treated her children, how she treated *everyone,* to know she was a good woman. The staff adored her.

"I also knew she wasn't happy. Before long I knew why. Caine treated her badly—like a possession, which is how he thought of her." He picked up his brandy glass and seemed surprised when it was empty.

"Do you want more?" Jack asked.

Brandon shook his head. "No, but I'd like a glass of water."

Jack went back to the pine chest, where he'd seen a pitcher of ice water earlier, and poured Brandon a glass. He poured himself more brandy.

When he was again seated, and Brandon had drunk some of his water, Brandon resumed talking. "I couldn't help myself. Before long, Madelyn and I were friends again. We started taking long walks together, talking about everything and anything, although we never discussed the past. Caine couldn't stand our friendship. He'd shown no real interest in Madelyn for years, because once he had something, he no longer wanted it, you see. The thrill was in the challenge of acquiring it. Yet when he saw that Madelyn and I were once more becoming close, he was furious."

Brandon sighed. "Neither Caine nor I knew it, but your mother was pregnant again. When your mother discovered the pregnancy and told Caine, he accused her of being pregnant with my child. He was so angry and so jealous he nearly hit her. Then he ordered us both out of his house. He told her he'd support her financially, but he never wanted to see her or her child again. He said if she tried to fight him on this, he would have her declared an unfit mother. He said he'd win in court, that no one would take her word over his.''

''And you believed this?'' Jack said skeptically.

''We were so stunned by Caine's accusations, we weren't really thinking. Plus, Madelyn was afraid for her children. She knew how Caine's mind worked and how irrational he could be when he was opposed. She knew he was perfectly capable of doing what he'd threatened to do. We decided we would wait for a while—let Caine calm down a bit.''

''So what happened?'' Jack asked. ''Why didn't you come back?''

''We tried. Well, I tried. We'd decided I should go alone, that if Madelyn was along it would only infuriate Caine and make him more unreasonable. At the time, we were in Houston. I decided it would be best to drive to Grandview, since we hoped I'd have you with me on the way back—you and your possessions.

''Just outside of Conroe, on a particularly bad stretch of the freeway, I had an accident. A van filled with college kids who had been drinking went out of control, jumped the median, and hit me head-on. I was badly injured, in the hospital for months. I underwent four surgeries. I still have a limp as a result of one of them. But the head injuries were the worst. I recovered, but my sight was mostly gone. By the time I was in any kind of shape to leave the hospital, Madelyn and I knew our chance to try to get you or the other children was gone. Caine had filed for divorce, accused Madelyn of adultery, as well as of emotional desertion, and with his money and power and connections, held all the cards.''

Brandon seemed totally spent by the effort of telling his story. Jack thought about everything Brandon had said. He was quiet for a long time. They both were. In the silence, Jack was aware of noises he hadn't noticed before: the ticking of the mantel clock, the faint squawk of the seagulls, the creaking of the house as the wind off the Sound picked up. Outdoors, it was nearly dark, and the street lamps had gone on. While Jack watched, a car drove slowly down the street.

''Jack?''

Jack sighed and turned his attention back to the man opposite him.

''Are you okay?''

''Yes.'' His voice sounded ragged to him, not like his voice at all.

''Do you have any questions?''

Jack had a million questions, but right now there

was only one he wanted answered. "Yes," he said in a stronger voice. "Where is my mother?"

Jack stared at the still-beautiful Madelyn, who sat so quietly in her studio, whose blue eyes were filled with such sorrow.

My mother. His heart pounded in his chest. *My mother.*

His gaze swung to Brandon, who had removed his dark glasses and whose nearly sightless eyes were pinned to Jack. *And my father.*

Jack swallowed, hard. He hadn't cried in years, not since he was eight years old, and the man he'd always believed was his father had refused to let him have a birthday party, even though his brothers and sister always had birthday parties. Yet at this moment, tears threatened, so close he was afraid if he didn't get out of there, away from those two pairs of pleading eyes, he might make a fool of himself.

Striding to the huge window that overlooked the water, he stared out. Moonlight silvered the water, illuminating the whitecaps that covered its surface. In the distance, he could see the running lights of several boats. It was a beautiful, tranquil setting, this place where his mother and father had lived for so long.

The pain that had always been with him, the pain he'd buried as deeply as possible so he would be able to survive, was now an open wound he could no longer pretend did not exist. Slowly he turned around to face Madelyn. "I understand why you left. I even understand why you didn't try to get custody of us. But why didn't you ever call? That's what I don't understand."

His mother sighed deeply. "I did try to call you," she answered softly. "Many times."

"And?"

"The housekeeper wouldn't put me through. I wrote to you, too, but the letters were always returned, unopened. Then Clyde Carlyle sent a note saying there was no use in me continuing to try to contact you and your brothers and sister. He said Caine would never allow it." She shook her head sadly. "Brandon thought we should take Caine to court, but I knew it was useless. Caine had done everything right. Despite the fact that he kicked me out of the house, technically, I'd abandoned you children. And with Caine's resources and our lack of resources at the time—the bulk of Brandon's money had gone to pay his medical bills—I knew I didn't stand a chance. Instead I begged Clyde to talk to Caine, to ask him to at least let me write to you and the others. Clyde said he'd do his best. A week later, he called. He said he was sorry, but Caine wouldn't budge. Neither Brandon nor I were to have any contact with any of you. If I tried to get around that, he would punish me by punishing you. *If you want your children to have a good life, you'll stay away.* Those were his exact words." Her throat worked, and her lovely eyes filled with tears. "Oh, Jack, my dearest son." She reached for his hand. "Please forgive me. I thought I was doing the best thing for you."

He looked at her hand, the long fingers, the delicate veins. Looked back at her face, the large eyes with the deep wells of sadness, the mouth so like Kate's, the thick hair that was now streaked with silver. He didn't want to forgive her. Didn't want to say he understood. And yet he knew Caine, knew how Caine could intimidate and frighten. "All right," he said coldly, pulling his hand away from hers. "That's why you didn't contact us when we young. But what about when we got older? Hell, I haven't lived under Caine's roof since I was eighteen. Even then, I was only there summers. You know he sent me away to military school, don't you?"

"Yes," she whispered brokenly. The tears spilled over, splashed down onto her mauve silk blouse, but she ignored them.

Jack didn't want to feel any sympathy for her. She wasn't the one who had been abandoned. He was!

She tried to speak, but her lips were trembling. Finally she managed to get herself under some kind of control. "After all those years went by, I..." She took a deep breath. "I thought you would hate me if you knew I wasn't dead, that I had given you up.

I thought you were better off without me." Now sobs racked her again.

"Madelyn, darling, don't." Brandon moved in her direction. He groped for her hand, clutching it tightly.

Jack still wanted to be angry. He still wanted to punish her—and Brandon—for all those lonely days and nights. For all those times Caine had belittled him. For all those instances when he'd doubted himself and his ability to love or be loved. And yet, that deep sadness in her eyes told him something. Something he really didn't want to know. She had suffered, too, maybe even more than he had. And even now, even if he forgave her and they forged some kind of relationship in the future, that sadness would probably never entirely disappear, because she would never be able to forget that she had abandoned her children—no matter the reason—and in so doing, she had given up something infinitely precious while denying them something that should be a child's inalienable right.

"I want you to know something, Jack," Brandon said quietly. "Your mother kept all those letters she wrote to you. And she kept writing them, too, even though they weren't mailed. There are hundreds of them upstairs, packed away in boxes. The same with your brothers and sister. Later, if you want, you can go up into the attic and bring them down. And if you read them, I think you'll see just how much she's always loved you. How you were never out of her thoughts.''

Jack's gaze swung back to Madelyn's. The love shining in her eyes nearly undid him.

''I love you,'' she said. Her tears ran unchecked down her cheeks. ''I've always loved you.''

With a muffled groan, he reached for her. And as they embraced, he finally allowed his own tears to come.

''Tell me about Beth,'' Madelyn said.

It was much later, nearly midnight. Brandon had gone to bed an hour before. So had Hope. The others—Cord, Rafe, Kate, and their respective partners had all headed back to the hotel. Only Jack had remained behind.

He smiled. ''She's amazing.''

His mother sat quietly, her eyes never leaving his face as he talked. A couple times she chuckled, especially when he told anecdotes about Amy and Matthew, but most of the time she just listened without comment.

''You love her,'' she said softly when he'd finished.

He nodded.

''Does she love you?''

''I don't know. I think she does.''

Madelyn smiled tenderly, reaching out to touch his cheek. ''How could she help but love you?''

Something akin to pain pierced Jack's heart. Her

words were the first words of praise he had ever heard from a parent. "There's a problem, though," he said gruffly, trying to cover up his emotional reaction. "When she finds out I've been lying to her all these weeks, she's going to be upset. She told me once that she detests liars."

"Oh, but surely, Jack, she'll forgive you."

"I hope so." But what if she didn't? What if she told him to get lost? He tried not to think of this possibility, because now that he'd found Beth, now that he knew the kind of life he *could* have, he wanted it desperately.

"Just be as honest with her as you can. Open your heart and tell her how you feel. Don't hold anything back. That's so important to a woman. To feel the man she loves trusts her with his deepest emotions."

"I hope you're right."

"I know I'm right."

They sat quietly for a while, just looking at each other, even though there were many things they hadn't talked about. Jack had hundreds of questions, but there was no real hurry. Now that they'd found each other again, they had the rest of their lives to talk.

"When you get everything worked out with Beth, will you bring her here to see us?"

"I'd like to," Jack said.

Madelyn smiled. "Isn't fate strange sometimes? I'll not only be gaining a daughter-in-law and two more grandchildren in addition to the adorable Becky, but you'll be the stepfather of your own distant cousins.''

Jack was taken aback by her statement until he realized she was right. It excited him to realize she was right. He had a blood connection to Beth's children. The children he already loved and wanted to help raise. Suddenly he felt more encouraged than he'd felt in days. Beth had to forgive him. They were meant to be together.

Beth was glad she'd gone to Dee Ann's for supper. The kids had enjoyed being there, too. She'd hardly thought about Jack at all, and when she had, it was with a good feeling. Dee Ann was right. Beth had jumped to conclusions and been worrying for nothing. Jack would be back. Maybe he'd even be back tomorrow.

She fell asleep with a smile on her face.

Chapter Twelve

Although Jack wished he could go back to Rose Hill on Monday, he needed to talk to Cord first. And then he was sure Cord would probably need a day or two to make the arrangements Jack wanted. Because it was very late when Jack got back to the inn Sunday night, he wrote Cord a note and slipped it under his door so he'd see it first thing in the morning.

Cord's call came at eight. Jack was awake, but he hadn't gotten out of bed yet.

"So how'd things go between you and our mother last night after we left?" Cord said.

"Good. Real good. We had a long talk."

"You still angry?"

Jack smiled. "No. Not anymore."

"Glad to hear it. You going back over there today? Hannah says we've been invited for lunch."

"Yes, but first I wanted to talk to you. There's something I need you to do for me."

"All right. Want me to come to your room?"

"Yes, but give me a half hour. I'll order some coffee from room service and take a quick shower."

"Order some sweet rolls, too."

Thirty-five minutes later the brothers sat on Jack's balcony, a small wrought-iron table between them. The room service waiter had just left. They each poured themselves a cup of coffee and Cord reached for a sweet roll. "All right," he said, "what's up?"

"I want you to arrange to have half of my share of Caine's inheritance put into a trust fund for Beth Johnson's children, and I want the other half to be transferred directly to Beth."

Cord stopped in mid-bite. "Are you *serious?*"

"Dead serious."

"But why?"

"Because even though we'll probably never be able to prove our grandfather swindled the Johnsons out of that land years ago, I feel in my gut that he did. So she and her kids have much more of a right to the money than I do. Besides," he added, "I never wanted the money."

"Jack, this is foolish."

''It's not. It's the smartest thing I've ever done.''

''Are you in love with this woman? Is that what's going on here?''

''Yes, but even if I wasn't in love with her, I'd still want to do this.''

''Look, I'm not trying to tell you what to do, but why don't you wait awhile? You might change your mind, and once that money's transferred or put in a trust, it'll be too late.''

''I won't change my mind.''

After ten more minutes of talking, Cord finally gave in. ''Hell, I can see it isn't any use trying to reason with you. Okay, fine. If you want to throw away a fortune, I'm not going to stop you. But I can't do this immediately, you know. The estate isn't liquid. It'll take me a couple of days to get the money together.''

''Fine. Once it's done, I want her to be officially notified by our attorney.''

''You don't want to tell her yourself?''

''I may. But I still want official notification.''

After Cord left to rejoin his wife and child, Jack felt lighter and freer than he'd felt in years. As soon as the transfer of money was complete, he would return to Rose Hill and tell Beth everything.

Jack hadn't prayed in a long time. But sitting there, looking out over the water, thinking about everything that had happened to him in the past two months, thinking about the incredible woman waiting for him in Rose Hill, he prayed that he would find the right words, that as his mother had said, Beth would understand…and forgive.

Jack had now been gone five days. Five days in which Beth tried to tell herself Dee Ann was right, that he'd said he'd be back, and he would. But each day without any word made it harder and harder for her to keep believing.

It had gotten so she dreaded facing the children when they came home from school, because the first thing they looked for was Jack's truck. And when they didn't see it, their faces fell in disappointment.

Since he'd left on Saturday afternoon, Beth had found it difficult to work, although there was plenty to be done. The trouble was, everywhere she looked she saw evidence of Jack's handiwork. The woodworking tools. The half-finished trellis he'd started making before he left. The half-dozen tripods that were ready for sale. The towels hanging in the little bathroom in the barn. The quilt draped over the daybed on the sleeping porch. Not to mention the images burned into her brain.

And if the days were difficult, the nights were almost impossible. Beth couldn't sleep. She tossed and turned, and when she finally did fall asleep, she was tormented by her dreams.

So after lunch on Thursday, she decided she would escape the farm and its memories and drive into Tyler for some needed supplies. She checked the misting system, adjusting it for the cloudiness of the day, stuffed her list into her purse and took off.

She made three stops—the hardware store, the supermarket, and then the rose growers' cooperative store where she bought her fertilizer and other business supplies at a discount. She was standing at the checkout, paying for her purchases, when Lou Castle, another small rose grower, walked in.

"Lou," she said, smiling happily for the first time in days. Lou was a favorite of hers; he'd been a good friend of her grandmother's. At seventy-six, everyone had expected him to retire long ago, but Lou loved his roses too much. He'd said he would work his farm until the day he died, and if he died among his roses, he'd die a happy man.

"Bethie, darlin', how are ya doin'?" Lou enveloped her in a bear hug. Because of the hard physical work he'd done for so long, his body was still muscled, still strong.

"I'm doing just fine, Lou. How have *you* been?"

"Oh, middlin'."

Beth smiled. *Middlin'* was his favorite answer whenever anyone asked how he was. "And Fanny?" Fanny was his wife of fifty-some years.

"Well, the arthritis in her knees is gettin' bad, but otherwise she's doin' good."

They talked a few minutes more, then Lou said, "I been meanin' to call you ever since we had that terrible storm back the beginnin' of September, but

I had a lotta damage myself, and then I heard you hired some help and were fixin' your place up, so I figured everythin' must be okay.''

"Yes, thank God for those low-interest government loans."

Lou frowned. "What loans?"

"Didn't you hear about it? The government was offering low-interest loans to any rose farmer who had storm damage. They probably still are."

"Heck, no, I didn't hear anything about that. Wonder why Kenny Berlin didn't mention it. I went in to talk to him about borrowin' some money, too. Where'd you get your loan?" Kenny Berlin was an officer of the bank in Rose Hill.

"I didn't go through the Rose Hill bank. This loan was arranged here in Tyler."

"That sure is strange. You'd have thought Kenny would know about somethin' like that. I'm gonna get on him."

Soon after, they said their goodbyes, and Beth took her purchases out to her truck. As she backed out of the parking lot, she kept thinking about her conversation with Lou. It was kind of strange that Kenny Berlin hadn't known about the low-interest loan available to Lou. Kenny was a sharp guy, a smart banker. Was it maybe Lou's age that was the problem?

Because the bank she'd dealt with was only a few blocks away from the cooperative, she decided she might as well swing by there and just ask the loan officer, that Harry Westerman, if there was some reason Lou wouldn't have been eligible for the same kind of loan she'd gotten. She'd have to hurry, though, so she'd be sure and be home in time to meet Amy's bus.

Luckily the bank was not busy. She headed for the glass-enclosed office where she'd signed her papers, but Harry Westerman wasn't in it. While she was trying to decide what to do, a pretty blonde in an elegant gray suit walked up to her.

"Hello. May I help you?"

"Yes. I got a loan here a few weeks back. Mr. Westerman was the loan officer I worked with, and I just wanted to ask him a couple of questions."

"I'm sorry. Mr. Westerman is on vacation. He won't be back until a week Monday." She smiled. "But I'm a loan officer. Maybe I can answer your questions. My name's Darian Sweet." She held out her hand.

"Beth Johnson."

The two women shook hands and Darian led Beth into the office next to Westerman's. "Have a seat," she said, indicating two floral upholstered chairs in front of a cherry wood desk. She walked around and sat behind the desk, then smiled at Beth again. "Now. What did you want to know?"

"Well, I was mainly just curious about whether a person's age would have made him ineligible for the kind of loan I got."

Darian frowned. "I'm not sure I understand. Age

really has nothing to do with most loans. It's the collateral that counts.''

"I know, but my loan was one of those low-interest, government-backed ones that were offered to rose growers who had storm damage in early September. We didn't have to put up any collateral to get it.''

The frown deepened. "Hmm. I don't believe I'm familiar with that particular type of loan.''

"Oh?'' Well, then maybe it wasn't so strange that Kenny Berlin hadn't mentioned the loan to Lou, if this woman wasn't familiar with it, either.

"But I can look it up,'' Darian said. She turned to her computer and began typing. "Is your first name Elizabeth?'' she said after a few minutes. "Elizabeth Lillian Johnson?''

"Yes, that's me.''

Darian studied the screen. She pursed her lips. "Hmm,'' she said again, frowning. Then she stood up. "I'm going to go pull your file.''

"Is something wrong?'' Beth said, alarmed.

"No, of course not. I just think maybe you misunderstood the terms of the loan. But let me get the file. Maybe *I'm* misunderstanding something.'' She walked out of the office, across the lobby and into another room. A few minutes later, manila folder in hand, she returned to the office. Sitting back down at her desk, she opened the folder, looked over a few pages, then closed the file. Her eyes met

Beth's. They were troubled. "I wish Mr. Westerman was here," she said.

"Then there *is* something wrong."

"Not with your loan. Everything here is in order. It's just that it's not a government-backed loan, and I'm not sure why you thought it was."

Beth's mouth dropped open. "What do you mean, it's not a government-backed loan?"

"It's not. It's what we call a personal-guarantee loan."

"A personal-guarantee loan?"

"Yes."

"What does that mean?"

Darian tapped her pen against the file. "It means someone has personally guaranteed that, should you default, he will cover the loan."

"What! Who would do that? And why would Mr. Westerman say the loan was government-backed?" Beth realized her voice had risen, but what Darian Sweet had just told her was incomprehensible.

"I'm not sure I should be telling you—"

"Is it or is it not my loan?" Beth demanded. Angrily she opened her purse and withdrew her wallet. "Here," she said, opening the wallet to the place where her driver's license was visible. "Look. There I am. Elizabeth L. Johnson."

"I don't doubt that you're whom you say you are," Darian said with dignity. "But since Mr. Westerman handled this, and he's not here…"

"I demand to see my file. If someone has given their personal guarantee that my loan will be repaid, I have a right to know who that person is." Beth glared at the woman across the desk, daring her to refuse.

Sighing, Darian said, "I'm sure there's some reasonable explanation for this, Mrs. Johnson, and when Mr. Westerman gets back, you can talk to him about it. In the meantime, the person who guaranteed your loan is Jack Stockwell."

"Jack Stockwell! Why, I don't even *know* Jack Stockwell." But the moment the words were out of her mouth, Beth knew they weren't true. Suddenly she was chilled to the bone. *Jack.* She shook her head, unable to believe it, yet knowing, down deep, that it was true. Her Jack, the Jack who said he was Jack Stokes—he hadn't even picked a name that was very different!—the same Jack who had been evasive about the places he'd lived and the things he'd done, was none other than a Stockwell.

Stunned, Beth stuffed her wallet back into her purse, and without even saying "good bye" or "thank you" or "kiss my foot" she blindly walked out of the office and out of the bank.

Beth's stomach churned. She had felt physically sick ever since she'd left the bank earlier that afternoon. She hadn't been able to eat supper or hide her distress from the children, even though she'd tried to do both.

Finally, though, they were both in bed and, she hoped, asleep.

She still couldn't believe it. Jack was a Stockwell. He had lied to her from the very first. She wondered if anything he'd said had been the truth.

Shame engulfed her every time she thought about making love to him. All the things she'd done and said. Had he been laughing at her? Thinking how stupid she was? Tears burned in her eyes, and she angrily swiped them away.

She would not cry! He wasn't worth crying over. He was a liar. A Stockwell. His family probably *had* stolen the Johnsons' land. And they were probably even now trying to steal *her* land. What other reason could there be for Jack to back her loan?

Oh, God. She really *was* stupid. She had hardly even read those loan papers, just let Westerman explain them to her and signed on the dotted line, just as she was told to. Why, for all she knew, Jack could take her land away from her anytime he wanted.

All these weeks while she had been spinning daydreams about a future with Jack, he had been after one thing and one thing only. Her farm!

When Jack reached Tyler, he started rehearsing what he would say when he saw Beth. He looked at the clock on the dash. It was after nine. He hoped Beth was still awake. If she wasn't, if the house was dark, he wouldn't frighten her by pulling into the driveway. He would just drive on past and go to the Temple Motel in Rose Hill. He didn't *want* to wait until morning to see her, but it wouldn't kill him if he had to. After all, he'd waited thirty-five years for Beth, he could wait a few hours more.

Damn! There were no lights on in the house. Jack sat in the truck and wished he knew if she was already asleep. Should he take a chance? Maybe turn the truck lights out and slowly drive up to the house?

No. He'd frighten her. Hell, she might go get her shotgun. Damn. He should have called her. Told her he was coming. Why hadn't he?

Well, it was too late now.

Maybe it was better to wait until morning to see her, anyway. The kids were there tonight, and if she got upset, they might wake up. Jack sure didn't want the kids to hear him and Beth arguing.

Reluctantly he turned his truck around and headed for Rose Hill.

Beth woke up with a raging headache, the result of crying herself to sleep. Even though she'd told herself she wasn't going to cry, she hadn't been able to keep the tears at bay. Tiptoeing downstairs, she put on the coffee and took some more pain-killer.

The sun was just coming up. The eastern sky was tinged with rose and gold. It was supposed to be a beautiful fall day, the kind that normally made her happy to be alive. But this morning she wasn't happy about anything. She wasn't sure she'd ever be truly happy again.

Why did she have such lousy judgment when it came to men? Was she more like her mother than she'd ever realized?

By the time the coffee was done, it was time to wake up the kids. She tried to empty her mind while she fixed their breakfast and the lunches she'd forgotten to get ready the night before.

"Don't you feel good, Mama?" Amy asked when Beth set her bowl of oatmeal in front of her.

"I'm fine," Beth lied. She forced a smile to her face. "Eat up, sweetie. You don't want to be late."

She was very glad when it was time for the children to leave. She had no energy for pretense, and she certainly didn't want them to know how miserable she was. After seeing them both safely onto their buses, she walked slowly back to the propagation house to start the first day of the rest of her life without Jack.

Beth heard the crunch of gravel and knew someone was coming up the driveway. She rinsed her hands under the faucet in the propagation house, then walked outside. Squinting against the sun, she headed around the house.

Suddenly her heart lurched, then began to pound. She couldn't believe her eyes.

Jack. Jack was climbing out of his truck. The sun glinted off his dark hair as he reached for his duffel.

For a moment, she forgot what had happened the day before, and happiness surged through her. Then, like a blow to the solar plexus, remembrance returned. Beth stopped in her tracks.

He swung the duffel out and turned. Their gazes locked. ''Beth!'' he called. He broke into a smile, started walking toward her.

Beth swallowed. How could he look so happy? Didn't it bother him that he was a liar? That he was deceiving her? Leading her to believe he was something he wasn't?

''Beth?'' he said as he drew closer. ''Is something wrong?''

She stared at him.

''Beth?'' he said again. He reached out to touch her.

Beth jerked away from his hand. She backed up.

''What is it, Beth?'' Now his voice held alarm.

''Get out,'' she said through clenched teeth. ''Get back in your truck and get out of here.''

''*What?*''

She put her hands over her ears. ''I don't want to hear one word out of your lying mouth, Jack *Stockwell.*''

It took a few seconds for her words to register, and when they did, he nodded. ''So that's it. How did you find out?''

''I went to the bank in Tyler, that's how! I

wanted to ask Westerman some questions. Only he wasn't there. But there was a very helpful woman. She pulled out my file for me. And that's how I found out that there was never any such thing as a government-backed loan! That my loan had been arranged by one Jack Stockwell. It wasn't very hard to put two and two together. I'm not *completely* stupid, despite what you might think!''

"I don't think you're stupid, Beth. I know it looks bad, but I was going to tell you. It's just that I had to wait until after I came back from Cape Cod. That's where I've been. To see my mother."

"You know what? I don't give a damn where you've been. In fact, I don't believe anything you have to say. I told you once how I feel about liars, and you're the worst liar I've ever come across! Now get out of here. And don't come back!''

Chapter Thirteen

Jack stared at Beth's rigid back as she disappeared into the propagation house. If she thought he was going to leave without ever giving him a chance to explain, she was wrong. He wasn't going anywhere.

However, he did feel a bit foolish standing there with his duffel bag in hand, so he walked back to his truck, threw the duffel inside, then followed her.

She was standing in front of the controls to the misting system. Although she was staring at the unit, it was obvious to him she was only pretending to study it, for her face was set in tight lines and her eyes were bright with angry tears. Her head whipped around as he walked inside. "I thought I told you to get out of here."

"I'm not leaving until we talk."

"We're not going to talk."

"Beth, don't be unreasonable. Let me—"

"There's nothing you could say that would make me feel any different than I feel now, so you might as well save your breath." Two bright spots of color dotted her cheeks.

"Even a condemned man is allowed to say his piece," Jack said softly. Then, effecting a disappointed tone, he added, "I guess I was wrong about you."

"And what's *that* supposed to mean?"

"I thought you were a fair person. That you'd keep an open mind—give a person a chance to tell his side of a story."

"A chance to manipulate me, you mean. Just like you've been doing for weeks."

"I don't know why you would say that. Okay, so I wasn't truthful about my real identity or who was responsible for your loan, but I *couldn't* tell you who I was up front, and you know it. You'd have run me off your land with a shotgun if you'd known I was a Stockwell."

"Damn right I would have!"

Beth never swore, so the strong language was an indication of just how distraught she was. It hurt Jack to see her so unhappy and to know he was the cause of that unhappiness. He *had* to make her listen! "And the reason I lied about the loan," he continued doggedly, "was because I know how proud you are. I knew you would never accept money from me, so I had to find a way to help you where you wouldn't know where the money had come from.''

"*Help* me? You mean you had to find a way to steal my land!''

"Steal your land? That doesn't make sense. How could I steal your land? Your land isn't collateral against the loan.'' It was only there an instant, but Jack saw the flash of uncertainty in her eyes, and he pressed harder. "If you default on the loan, the only thing that'll happen is I'll lose the money I put up. There's no way I could get your land. Hell, Beth, read your loan papers. I defy you to show me where it says anything about your land.''

For a moment, she just glared at him. "Well, just what *do* you want, Jack? Why did you come here in the first place?''

"I came because I wanted to try to find out if your husband's family's claims concerning that land my family acquired from his had any merit. If there might be some proof that we had swindled them.''

"Why didn't you just ask? Why did you have to lie to me?''

Jack sighed. "You know, Beth, as much as I wish I could have been honest with you from the beginning, I'm not sorry I did what I did.''

"Oh, that doesn't surprise me,'' she said bitterly.

"Rich people always think they're above the rules."

"I don't think I'm above the rules. The reason I said I wasn't sorry is that if I had told you who I was in the beginning, I would never have had the opportunity to live here and work here. I'd have never gotten to know you and Matthew and Amy. And getting to know you and the kids is the best thing that's ever happened to me. It's shown me a different way of life, one I never thought was a possibility for me. It's given me hope for the future." His voice lowered. "I love you, Beth. Don't you know that?"

She had put her hands over her ears and was shaking her head.

"Don't shake your head. It's true. I love you. I've loved you almost since the beginning, although I didn't realize it until recently. I want to marry you and stay here forever. I want us to be a family."

"Once I would have been thrilled to hear you say that, Jack. But now it's too late. You lied to me. How can I ever believe you or trust you again?" She bowed her head. "I want you to leave."

Jack stared at her bowed head. He was frustrated. What could he say to get through to her? "I'm not leaving. The only way you'll get me off this property is to call the police and have me thrown off. And until you do, I'm going to work." So saying, he strode off in the direction of the barn.

* * *

Beth was dumbfounded. What did he think he was doing? This was *her* farm, not his. And if she wanted him gone, he was going. Did he think she *wouldn't* call the police? Did he think, just because she'd been a pushover once, she would continue to be? Furiously she swiped away her tears and, after a moment's indecision, stalked into the house.

It took thirty minutes—thirty minutes of righteous pacing and muttering—before Tubby Richards, the lone law enforcement officer of Rose Hill, pulled into her driveway in his shiny new police cruiser. Beth had been watching for him and, the moment he opened his car door, she walked out onto her front porch.

"It's about time you got here," she said.

"What seems to be the trouble, Beth?" he said as he levered himself out of the car. True to his name, his belly was straining against his blue shirt.

"There's a man in the barn. I asked him to leave, and he refused."

Tubby frowned. "Who is he?"

"Someone who used to work for me. Would you just get him off my property, please?"

"Okay, Beth. Now don't get all excited. I got it under control." He started off toward the barn, then suddenly stopped. "Has he got a gun?" He fingered his own gun nervously.

"No. He's not dangerous. I just don't want him here."

Nodding, Tubby disappeared around the corner. Five minutes later, he reappeared with Jack. They were talking and laughing like old friends.

Beth glared at them.

When they saw her, they fell silent. Tubby, who had removed his hat, scratched his head. Clearing his throat, he said, "Um, Beth, don't you think you two can work this out? Mr. Stockwell here says he, um, loves you, and you two just had a misunderstanding."

Beth wanted to scream. She hated all men. What were they good for, anyway? You couldn't count on a single one of them. She was ashamed that she'd wasted a single tear on any man, ever. "That's not the way I see it," she said as calmly as she could manage. "This is my farm, and *Mr. Stockwell* is not welcome here. He's trespassing, and I want you to *make him leave.*"

"Now, Beth," Tubby said.

"Don't do this, Beth," Jack said.

She crossed her arms in front of her chest. "He's trespassing," she repeated, glaring at Tubby. "And if *you* can't do anything about it, I'll go get my shotgun and take care of this myself!"

Tubby sighed and looked at Jack. "I'm sorry, Mr. Stockwell."

Jack shrugged.

Beth turned her back on both of them and marched back into the house. She didn't know which of them she was more disgusted with. Lying

Jack. Or fawning Tubby, who was all but salivating over the Stockwell name. Well, good riddance to both of them.

A few minutes later, she heard car and truck doors thunking shut, followed by first one, then the other ignition catching. When she finally heard the sound of tires crunching on gravel, she trembled violently, and no matter how much she didn't want to, no matter how many times she told herself she was the biggest fool on earth, she couldn't stop the flood of tears from coming.

When the phone rang an hour later, Beth almost didn't answer it. She just didn't have the strength to talk to anyone. But then she remembered that it could be the school calling about one of the kids, and she picked up the phone.

"Beth?"

"Yes?"

"Beth, this is Kenny Berlin. With the Rose Hill bank."

"Oh. Hi, Kenny. For a second, I didn't recognize your voice. What can I do for you?"

"Well, I just wanted to assure you that the money was wired to your account yesterday afternoon and tell you that I'm available anytime you want to talk about investments. I know you won't want to leave a sum this large just sitting here."

Beth frowned. "What are you talking about? What money?"

For a moment, he didn't answer. Then, cautiously he said, "You know. Your share of the Stockwell estate."

"My share of the Stockwell estate?" Beth was so flabbergasted she had to sit down.

"Yes. Needless to say, we are very happy you have chosen us to oversee this money. I don't think our bank has ever had a deposit that approaches this amount." He went on to name an eight-figure total that made Beth gasp. "And as I said, anytime that's convenient for you, I'll be happy to meet with you and discuss what type of investments you're interested in pursuing."

Beth sat and stared at the phone after Kenny said goodbye. Twenty-five million dollars? It was such a ridiculously large sum of money, she couldn't even absorb it. There had to be some mistake. This couldn't be true. Why would the Stockwell family give *her* any money? If that phone call hadn't come from Kenny Berlin, someone she knew and trusted, she would have figured the call was a hoax. But Kenny Berlin had sounded so certain. He'd also sounded so *respectful*, the way people did when they were talking to someone wealthy and important. A way Beth had never been talked to in her life. That, more than anything else, told her this was true. She had been given a share of the Stockwell estate to the tune of twenty-five million dollars. And the reason had to have something to do with Jack.

Ten minutes later, she was on her way to the Temple Motel in Rose Hill.

Jack knew Beth would figure out where he was staying. He also knew she would seek him out as soon as she'd heard from her bank and knew about the money. Well, *half* the money, anyway.

Sure enough, less than two hours after he'd left the farm, she pulled into the parking lot of the Temple Motel.

"Here comes Bethie," Mr. Temple said. He and Jack had been talking in the motel office. "She comin' to see you?"

Jack smiled. "Yes. See you later, Mr. Temple." And then he walked outside.

"What's going on, Jack?"

It was all Jack could do to keep from yanking her into his arms and kissing her senseless. "What do you mean?"

"Don't play dumb. You know what I mean. Why has an obscene amount of money been deposited into my account at the Rose Hill bank?"

"Because it's your rightful share of the Stockwell estate."

"I am *not* a Stockwell. I don't *have* a share in the Stockwell estate."

"You do now," he pointed out.

"I don't want it."

"Look, Beth. If you don't want it, give it away.

You can do anything you want with that money, because whether you like it or not, it's yours. And you might as well know something else. That twenty-five million dollars you think is so obscene? It's only half of the amount that has been decided belongs to the Johnson family. The other half, another twenty-five million dollars, is now in an irrevocable trust for Amy and Matthew.''

Her mouth fell open, and for the first time since Jack had returned this morning, she seemed totally incapable of speech, angry or otherwise.

''You see, my father, oops, correction, the man I *thought* was my father, had amassed a fortune of more than three billion dollars. Your share came to fifty million, half for you outright and half for your children. You'll be hearing from the trustee of their account, probably within a day or so. Now, you can give away your portion of the money, but you can't touch Amy's and Matthew's. That money will be theirs to share when they turn twenty-five.''

Somewhere in the fog created by the unbelievable things he was telling her, Beth heard *the man I thought was my father*. She wet her lips. ''The…the man you thought was your father?''

Jack slowly smiled. ''Does that question mean you're ready to sit down and quietly talk?''

''I—I don't know what it means. I can't think.'' But all the fight had gone out of her, because as betrayed as she'd felt just minutes ago, and as much as she wanted to keep believing Jack was not to be trusted, even she knew no man would arrange to give a woman and her children fifty million dollars if he wished her harm. It was too big a gesture. It said she was important to him, whether she wanted to be or not.

"Beth, sweetheart, why don't we go back to the farm? We can sit down and talk. You can ask me anything you want, and I promise you..." He touched his heart. "I promise you I will tell you everything."

Beth swallowed.

"I love you, Beth. Until I met you, I didn't think I'd ever love anyone like this or that they would love me. *Could* love me. But that's all changed now, and the credit goes to you. I want to spend the rest of my life with you on your rose farm. I want to work alongside you, and have babies with you, and help you raise Amy and Matthew. I want us to be together until we're old and decrepit." His blue eyes blazed with intensity.

She'd always known those eyes of his would be her undoing. "Oh, Jack..."

"I love you so much, Beth."

"Oh, Jack," she cried. "I love you, too." And then she threw herself into his arms and lost herself in his kiss.

"A mercenary? Are you serious?"

Jack grimaced. "Yes. For the past fourteen years."

Beth shook her head. "But Jack, how could you do something like that? I mean, I don't know much, but even I know that mercenaries aren't exactly honorable people."

"Some of them are." He went on to explain how he only worked for causes he believed in and how he'd specialized in hostage rescue. "A few years ago I was responsible for getting a dozen children away from a madman who was holding them until the president of his country was beheaded on the steps of the capitol."

For a long moment, she sat silently. Then, in a voice filled with wonder, she said, "There's so much we don't know about each other, isn't there?"

Until that moment, Jack hadn't realized how tense he was, how much he had dreaded her reaction to his revelation about his past life. Feeling as if a weight had been lifted, he snuggled her closer. "But we have the rest of our lives to talk."

Lifting her face to his, she smiled into his eyes.

One week later...

"Beth, I just can't believe you did all this in one week!" Dee Ann exclaimed.

"It wasn't easy," Beth said. The two women were in Beth's bedroom, and Dee Ann was putting the finishing touches on Beth's hairdo. It was the morning of Beth's wedding day—a brilliant, crisp

October day. "But money *does* smooth the way,"
she said dryly. It was amazing how quickly she'd
gotten used to the idea of having money.

"Oh, Beth, this is all like a fairy tale," Dee Ann
gushed. "You know, Cinderella."

Beth grinned. "'Cinderella Meets The Mercenary'?"

"Something like that."

Beth still had moments when it was hard to believe that Jack, her Jack, had been a mercenary in
his former life. "I never thought you were a romantic, Dee Ann."

"Oh, you did, too. I've always talked a good
game, but down deep I'm just like every other
woman on the planet. We're *all* romantics. We all
want a handsome prince." She sighed. "And you
got the handsomest one of all!" Sighing again, she
picked up a bottle of hair spray and gave Beth's
hair a spritz. "There. You look gorgeous."

Beth looked at herself in the mirror. She did look
good. Dee Ann had put her hair up, pulling out just
a few curly tendrils at the sides of her face. Later,
closer to the three-o'clock ceremony, which would
take place in the side yard, Dee Ann would weave
yellow roses into the hairdo. Beth's wedding dress
was yellow, too. Yellow lace. It was the most beautiful dress she'd ever owned, and even though her
frugal nature had balked at the thought of spending
that much money on a dress, she hadn't been able
to resist it. It had the kind of old-fashioned charm

that had always beguiled Beth, with a high neck-line, long sleeves and a form-fitting torso. The skirt fell in graceful layers and was a flattering tea length. With it she would wear cream-colored stockings and matching satin shoes.

Her bouquet—which she'd fashioned herself—was a nosegay of yellow-and-flame colored roses.

"What time are Jack's folks arriving?" Dee Ann said, plopping down on Beth's bed.

"At two." Beth tried to quell the butterflies that any mention of Jack's family brought on. She was so nervous about meeting them, even though he'd told her she would like them all.

"Not a one of them is a snob," he'd assured her. "Cord likes expensive cars and clothes, but he's just like you or me. And you'll love Hannah. She's a real sweetheart. And little Becky's a doll." He went on to describe the rest of his siblings and their spouses or about-to-be spouses.

"But will they like *me?*" she'd worried. After all, she wasn't educated or to the manor born.

"They'll *love* you," he'd said, kissing her neck. "Who could help but love you?"

"Oh, you're just prejudiced."

"Damn right I am."

After that, they didn't talk much because neck kissing had led to other kinds of kissing, which had led to even more pleasurable activities. Remembering, Beth smiled.

"Oh, every time you get that Mona Lisa look on

your face, I'm so *jealous!*" Dee Ann cried. "I know exactly what you're thinkin' of."

"Oh, Dee Ann, I'm so happy."

Dee Ann eyes softened. "I know you are, hon, and I'm happy for you. You deserve this."

Beth wasn't sure what she'd done to deserve so much, but she wasn't going to quibble with fate. She had always counted her blessings, and now she would just count them more often. "Thanks."

Dee Ann grinned. "You're welcome. Now. Let's get you dressed, Mrs. Stockwell-to-be."

"You're everything Jack said you were."

Jack's heart swelled with pride as he watched his mother and Beth embrace.

"Thank you, Mrs. LeClaire."

"Oh, please. Let's not be formal. Call me Madelyn. After all, we're practically related. You know, I *am* related to your children."

Beth's eyes met Jack's, and he knew she was remembering when she'd first realized he and Amy and Matthew shared some of the same bloodlines and how happy that had made her. They'd had a long talk afterward, and he had told her he'd been thinking about it and wanted to adopt Amy and Matthew. She had thrown her arms around him and started to cry. Once more, as he had so many times over the past week, he wanted to pinch himself. Make sure all this was really happening to him.

As he stood watching, Beth was introduced to

the rest of his siblings. He could see she felt a bit overwhelmed by them—they were a colorful, larger-than-life bunch—but she would soon get used to them.

"Beth," Dee Ann said, looking at her watch. "It's time to get ready."

Beth nodded, said her goodbyes to his family and, for a second, her eyes met his. No words were spoken, but her eyes relayed the same message he knew his were telling her: *I love you.*

When she and Dee Ann had disappeared upstairs, Jack began to herd his family outdoors. Folding chairs had been set up in the side yard, facing a trellis that was covered with pink roses—Jack had already forgotten their name—but they were a species that bloomed repeatedly until the first frost, Beth had told him.

By the time Hannah and Becky and Caroline and Kate and Jack's mother and father and Hope were all seated, other guests had begun to arrive. Rafe and Brett were acting as ushers, and Cord was going to be Jack's best man. Jack had almost asked Brandon if he would act in that capacity, but then he'd realized Brandon would be uncomfortable and nervous about losing his footing in unfamiliar surroundings, so Jack decided on Cord.

Most of the guests were Beth's friends from Rose Hill and the surrounding Tyler area. Only a few were Jack's. He had been gone too long to have maintained many friendships.

At two forty-five, the minister from Beth's church arrived, followed closely by the string quartet Jack had hired. After greeting Jack, Reverend Andrews took his place behind the trellis. The musicians arranged themselves to the left side, unpacked their instruments and began to tune up.

They couldn't have ordered a more beautiful day, Jack thought. The sky was cloudless and that pure blue that only seems to happen in the autumn months. The temperature hovered around sixty-five, and a gentle breeze wafted over the assembled guests, carrying the fragrance of all the fall-blooming roses. Happy conversation rippled through the guests, but as the string quartet began to play "Air" from Handel's *Water Music,* they quieted in honor of the lovely sounds of the violins, viola and cello.

As the last notes died away, there was an expectant hush. The musicians picked up their instruments; the leader nodded to Jack. Slowly Jack, followed by Cord, walked to the trellis, where he took his place on the right.

Just as he saw Beth and Dee Ann, followed by Matthew and Amy, emerge from the house and slowly make their way down the porch steps and over the carpet that had been laid to protect the bride's shoes, the first strains of Mendelssohn's "Wedding March" filled the air.

Dee Ann, dressed in pale green, was the first to walk up the aisle. After her came Amy, in identical pale green, and she was followed by Matthew, who grinned at Jack.

Finally it was Beth's turn.

Jack's heart filled as he watched Beth, looking lovelier than he could ever have imagined, walk slowly up the aisle. Her smile was radiant, and as her eyes met his, he knew he would never forget this day.

When the music died away, Jack took Beth's hand, and together they faced the minister, who smiled at them. "We are gathered together on this beautiful day God has made to join in holy matrimony these two young people, John Brandon Stockwell and Elizabeth Lillian Johnson."

He continued on in his sonorous voice, talking to them about the sanctity of marriage and the promises they would soon make to each other.

And then it was time for their vows. Jack looked down into Beth's soft brown eyes and spoke the words they had written together. His heart swelled until he thought it might burst.

When it was Beth's turn, her voice rang out clear and firm. Her gaze locked with Jack's as she pledged her love and trust, and she knew that this moment, when she was promising herself to him, would forever be etched in her memory.

After the vows, Matthew proudly brought forth the ring Jack had selected only days earlier. A wide platinum band studded with three rows of diamonds, it was breathtaking. Beth looked at it and felt as if she were floating in a dream world. Yet never in her wildest dreams had she ever imagined a day like this or a man like Jack.

"I now pronounce you husband and wife," Reverend Andrews said with a beatific smile. He looked at Jack. "You may kiss the bride."

Beth sighed as Jack's lips met hers, and around her, the guests sighed, too, and many of them wiped tears from their eyes. Madelyn was openly crying, as were Kate and Hannah. Even Cord seemed misty-eyed, and Brandon was obviously affected, for he kept blowing his nose.

Madelyn, clutching her husband's hand, was thinking how long she had hoped and dreamed of this day and despaired of ever being here to see it. Kate, holding equally tightly to Brett's hand, was thinking how much her brother deserved this happiness and how she hoped Beth would never hurt him. Hannah, watching Cord watch his brother, was thinking what a big old softie Jack was—just like Cord, actually—and that Cord hadn't ever really known his oldest brother until now. None of them had. Brandon, who was trying to get his emotions under control, was thinking how much he wished he could see his son, just once, and how grateful he was that he had finally been able to acknowledge him. And Cord, Cord was thinking maybe he'd been wrong. Maybe Jack *wasn't* crazy for giving up all that money. Maybe what he'd gotten in return was worth every penny.

After the kiss, the lovely bride and bemused groom walked hand in hand down the aisle amid watery smiles and happy cheers and clapping.

A huge tent had been set up at the front of the property, near Beth's rose garden. Following the newly married pair, the minister, the musicians and the guests made their way to the reception.

The next couple of hours were filled with music, laughter and good wishes. The buffet table was loaded with delicacies: smoked salmon, stuffed Portobello mushrooms, patés of every description, fat shrimp, razor-thin slices of prosciutto, luscious cheeses and crackers and rolls, all kinds of vegetables and fruits, miniature quiches and deviled eggs, pastries and nuts. Champagne flowed freely from an elaborate fountain, and everyone ate, drank and talked. Some even danced. When the quartet began to play the "Anniversary Waltz" Jack turned to Beth, held out his hand and said, "Shall we?"

"You dance, too?" Beth said with a teasing smile.

"I told you. I'm a man of many talents."

Beth rolled her eyes.

When Jack took Beth into his arms and pulled her close, he could hear the approving murmur of their guests. "They're all watching us," he said.

"I know."

"Does it bother you?"

"Today?" Her eyes caressed him. "Nothing bothers me today."

He pulled her closer and bent to murmur into her ear. "I can't wait until they all go. I can't wait until we're alone."

Beth's heart fluttered. She couldn't wait, either. "Soon," she said.

Jack wished he were taking her away somewhere, but they had decided to postpone a honeymoon until she could find a couple of trained men to take over the farm while they were gone. They were aiming for a November trip and had settled on Italy. Jack had already inquired about a villa in Tuscany and the owner had promised to hold it for him.

When the music ended, he didn't want to let her go. And suddenly, he decided he didn't have to. Where was it written that the bride and groom had to stay at the reception until the last guest left? Dee Ann and Cord and Rafe would oversee things, make sure the guests got off and the musicians were paid and everything was cleared out. And Dee Ann was taking Amy and Matthew home with her; their duffel bags were already packed and waiting.

So with a grin, Jack scooped Beth up, turned to the crowd and said, "Thank you all for coming. Stay as long as you like." Beth, after one startled look, smiled, too. Then she undid her bouquet, which she'd tied to her wrist, and tossed it over her shoulder.

Amid teasing laughter and shouts, the new Mr. and Mrs. Jack Stockwell left their guests and headed for their home and their bedroom, where they could hardly wait to begin the rest of their lives together.

* * * * *

Don't miss this exciting new Silhouette Special Edition series from Laurie Paige!

Twenty years ago, tragedy struck the Windoms. Now the truth will be revealed with the power—and passion—of true love! Meet Kate, Shannon and Megan, three cousins who vow to restore the family name.

THE WINDRAVEN LEGACY

On sale May 2001
A stranger came, looking for a place to stay—
but what was he really looking for…? Find out why
Kate has **SOMETHING TO TALK ABOUT.**

On sale July 2001
An accident robbed Shannon of her sight, but a
neighbor refused to let her stay blind about her
feelings…in **WHEN I SEE YOUR FACE.**

On sale September 2001
Megan's memories of childhood had been lost.
Now she has a chance to discover the truth about
love…**WHEN I DREAM OF YOU.**

Available at your favorite retail outlet.

Silhouette®
Where love comes alive™

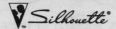

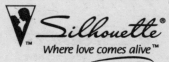

SILHOUETTE® MAKES YOU A STAR!

*Look in the back pages of
all June Silhouette series books to find an
exciting new contest with fabulous prizes!
Available exclusively through Silhouette.*

Don't miss it!

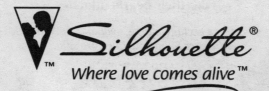

Silhouette®

Where love comes alive™

*P.S. Watch for details on how you can meet
your favorite Silhouette author.*

Award-winning, bestselling authors

Christine Rimmer & Laurie Paige

are known for their heartwarming, emotional stories of
family, children and the connections that grow between
couples. Here are two compelling stories about
marriages of convenience....

DOUBLE DARE
They'd known each other forever and Casey and Joanna
married to keep custody of his nephew. But sharing a life, a
family...a *bed*...wasn't like anything they'd ever expected....

MOLLY DARLING
He knew his tiny daughter needed a mother—and that
Molly would shower Lass with tender care. But what
happened when Sam realized he wanted Molly's love,
tenderness and *passion* for himself?

Come see how

Convenient Vows **become anything but**
convenient in May 2001.

Available wherever Silhouette books are sold!